KNIGHT

OF

South Holland

Book 3 of the Knights of the Castle Series

Karen D. Bradley

Ambrosia Sands Books
Dolton, Illinois

Ambrosia Sands Books
PO Box 827
Dolton, IL 60419
www.ambrosiasands.com

Knights of South Holland © Copyright 2020 by Karen D. Bradley
Trade Paperback ISBN: 978-1-7336089-5-4
Digital ISBN: 978-1-7336089-4-7
Library of Congress Control Number: 2020911679

Cover Art by: Woodson Creative Studios www.woodsoncreativestudio.com
Interior Design by: Lissa Woodson www.naleighnakai.com
Manufactured and Printed in the United States of America

Editors: J. L. Campbell jlcampbellwrites@gmail.com; Lissa Woodson, Brynn Weimer, Stephanie M. Freeman
Betas: Debra J. Mitchell, Kelsie Mitchell, Brynn Weimer, and Ellen Kiley Goeckler

KNIGHT

OF

South Holland

Book 3 of the Knights of the Castle Series

Karen D. Bradley

♦ DEDICATION ♦

To all the Kings and Queens who suffer in silence but keep their heads up and fight for their better tomorrow.

♦ ACKNOWLEDGEMENTS ♦

To my family and friends and core group of readers, thanks for supporting me through the ups and downs of this unexpected writing expedition. Most of what I have accomplished has been due to your excitement and encouragement that has provided fuel for a journey I wasn't sure was mine to take.

A special shout out to my sister, Jenetta M. Bradley, for her part in getting my books off the shelf where they were collecting dust. I appreciate you reading my stories over and over again without complaint.

English and Grammar were never my strongest subjects but the stories in my head didn't seem to care about that fact. Thanks to my editor Lissa Woodson (Naleighna Kai) for your energy and efforts in strengthening the weakness in my writing, challenging me to be better and improving the novel.

To Ellen Kiley Goeckler, Brynn Weimer, Kelsie Maxwell, and Debra Mitchell, I appreciate your time and assistance. Your comments, corrections and questions were essential to putting the final touches to the story.

A special thanks to J. L. Woodson for doing what you do best.

Finally, thank you to everyone who purchases a book. Know that your support is appreciated.

Karen D. Bradley

Chapter 1

The devil is coming echoed in every corner of Calvin Atwood's mind.

The thought freaked him out a bit. His mentors always encouraged him to focus so his mind was stronger than his feelings. Unfortunately, he couldn't shake the sensation trouble was heading his way that would send his world spiraling off its axis.

"You okay?" Mia Jakob held the mauve lipstick away from her luscious lips as she glanced over at him.

"Yes." Calvin gave her a half-smile before pulling in front of The Hilton. "I can't believe my parents are actually in Chicago."

"This is the first time since your brother's death, right?" Mia ran her long, tapered fingers through dark tresses that spilled over her shoulder before closing the visor.

"Sounds about right," he answered, trying to tamp down the anger that surfaced when the thought came that his brother would still be alive if Calvin's invention had been finished and in the hands of the right people.

His parents, Bruce and Janine Atwood, were in town for a fundraising event for families of the men who were lost during an attempt to rescue hostages in the middle of a military operation overseas. His brother, Shawn, was one of the men who didn't make it home. Losing him was the reason Calvin created the Emperor's Suit Project, an invention which camouflaged the wearer by making them appear invisible to the naked eye. Something that would have afforded Shawn the opportunity to execute their orders and make it back to American shores in one piece.

Earlier that year, Calvin had planned to sell the device to the American government. Unfortunately, someone he once trusted linked up with a partner intent on lining his own pockets by selling it to the highest bidder. When several assassins made attempts to take Calvin and the device he called The Emperor's Suit, he then required twenty-four hour protection. Mia, a top security specialist, had been assigned to the job. That situation made him rethink the project and whose hands he would place it in, because the American government's hands weren't so clean, either.

The Kings of the Castle had proven trustworthy and now their organization would benefit not only from that project, but also personal shields and a few other devices Calvin had in the works.

"I'm hoping that us being here will bring the right vibe." Calvin left the car, quickly bypassed the uniformed man to open Mia's door, taking in her heart-shaped face and the light dusting of cosmetics which highlighted her natural beauty. Then his gaze lowered to the emerald lace dress that hugged her shapely figure. Some days he couldn't believe the woman who was hired by a top security firm to be his "wife", was now his actual fiancée. She enriched his life in the most unexpected ways.

He could feel several pairs of eyes on them the moment they hit the pathway leading to the hotel. Maybe he was being overly cautious, but he didn't think so. Mia, a trained security specialist, had also scanned the area several times, thinking that he wouldn't catch her movements. He was more in tune with her than she realized.

"Dinner and dancing should keep things from getting too heavy." Mia's heels clicked over the cement as they moved toward the revolving door.

"Let's hope," Calvin said, as they made their way past the upscale bar area not far from the front desk. "Did I mention that you look gorgeous and incredibly sexy tonight?"

She gave him a radiant smile that made her even more beautiful. "Yes, several times."

If Calvin had had his way, they would be in bed doing that age-old dance that brought a world of pleasure. That thought was cut short because his parents were standing in front of a golden staircase which led up to the ballroom when they arrived. Janine's grey locs were in a braided bun. She wore a navy sequined pants suit. She gathered Mia in a warm embrace before doing the same to Calvin. "It's so great to see you."

"Miracles do happen." Bruce, who wore a pinstriped suit that complemented his wife's outfit, pulled Calvin into an embrace. "My son's out on a work night. That's a first and probably a world record somewhere."

"Now can you make sure he pencils us in for brunch on Saturday?" Janine looped her arm into Mia's before heading up to the ballroom.

"Mom," Calvin warned with a smile. It had been ages since he'd seen his parents seem genuinely happy.

"What?" She pinned him with a look that used to stop him in his tracks. "We haven't been in Chicago in a while, but even when we were living here you were always too busy working to see us."

Calvin resisted the urge to inform them that during several times when they had arrived unexpectedly, he was under government quarantine while working on a project and had been forbidden to make contact with any outside sources. If his mother knew how dangerous his line of work truly was, she would worry unnecessarily.

The ballroom had a massive dance floor in the center with a mix of black and silver cocktail, banquet, and café tables on the outer edges. An array of delicacies and chef stations were spread out on the north and south ends of the room as well as a total of four fully-stocked bars scattered throughout the space. The theme for tonight seemed to be travel, as evidenced by global landmark centerpieces, luggage tag confetti and the image of a world map projected on the wall behind the deejay booth.

"How long are you in town?" Mia glanced back at him giving him a knowing smile, as she veered his mother away from a sensitive conversation and to a table.

Bruce pulled a chair out for Janine at the same time Calvin did the same for Mia. "We're here for a little over a week, then we're heading to Lake Geneva to raise money for military families before heading back to Florida."

"That sounds awesome," Mia said, but Janine barely heard her as the older woman took Calvin's hand. "We wanted to talk to you about—"

Bruce leaned in, whispering, "Not now honey."

The tone, which carried a stark warning, caused Mia and Calvin to share a confused glance.

Mason Jakob, Mia's father, had a towering physique that commanded attention as he wound his way through the people and appeared at the table seconds later. "Lovely seeing you again," he greeted the Atwoods, gave Mia a peck on the cheek and shook Calvin's hand before taking a seat.

"Perfect timing." Janine lifted the water pitcher from the center of the table and poured some into her glass and then her husband's. "I was about to ask them about this wedding that they can't seem to find time to plan because of their busy schedules."

The way his mother twisted her lips to the side when she spoke let Calvin know that the wedding wasn't the original topic she had planned to discuss. What was going on with his parents?

"Janine." Bruce nodded toward the buffet and the line growing past the first section of tables. "Let them be, at least until after we eat."

Calvin waited for his parents to return before leaving the table to fix a plate for Mia and himself. The conversation was light with them exchanging funny stories about youthful antics, family, and encounters with those they termed "crazy people". All of them had enough of those in their lives to keep the conversation going until the end of next week.

"Come on Bruce." Janine shifted her chair back, nodded toward the few people gliding across the dance floor to *Love's Gonna Last* by British R&B artist, Jeffree. "Let's show these young bucks how Chicago Style Stepping is done."

Calvin smiled as his parents slid onto the dance floor. They used to throw parties and dance all night, but he'd been too busy reading science books and creating intricate devices to participate. He hadn't realized what he'd missed out on until his brother's death, when his parents became consumed with grief. They had lost a little of themselves then, and only later did he realize that they mostly feared losing him too.

The plan when he first left home was to come early because in another couple of hours the ballroom would be packed and hard to navigate. However, with the work ahead of him tomorrow, he planned to be home curled up next to Mia by then. He thought his parents would be of that same mindset, but they were acting more like their old selves again. That meant they would be out on the dance floor until they shut the place down. Happiness radiated from them, and Calvin could only hope that his relationship with Mia would survive the trials and tribulations that came with a love so strong.

"Let's join them." Calvin guided Mia from her seat and she smiled up at him, always elated when he indulged in something other than having his nose in a project or sequestered in his lab. He had already been put on notice that being all-consumed when it came to one area of his life, didn't leave room for her to be in the other areas that mattered just as well.

The ordeal and betrayal that nearly cost their lives, and the need to live in a less populated and safer area, led to purchasing a home together in the South Holland area. Calvin and Mia had taken Stepping classes at the Dorchester in Dolton; learning the smooth dance style that combined swing, bop, and a slowed down derivative of the jitterbug. This also led to them renting a hotel room in downtown Chicago a couple of nights to participate in Summer Dance in Grant Park where they enjoyed Salsa, Kizomba as well as Stepping. From movies, theatre, dancing, long walks on the lake, Calvin was living his life full out and loving it.

Even though they hit some rough spots over the last few months—

mostly due to a new couple with strong personalities finding their way together, it only reminded him to not only appreciate life but also cherish it. Having several close brushes with death could do that. The fact that Mia also had nearly lost her own life in the process of protecting him and his project, gave him a greater appreciation of having her by his side.

"What?" His mother's eyes went wide as they moved in to dance beside his parents.

Calvin mimicked his mother's reaction, causing her to giggle, before his eyes drifted back to the table. No surprise that Mason already had someone—actually, three women—keeping him company. The widower always drew his share of female attention. Not that he would take them up on it, but he could flirt with the best of them.

Three songs in, Janine tapped Mia's shoulder as Bruce slid off to the side. "I have to dance with my son. You've got him dancing like a champ. I see it, but have to experience it to believe it."

Mia tried to hide a laugh and Calvin gave her the evil eye before she swept past them to join Bruce and Mason at the table. A couple of songs later only Mason and Mia were still seated.

"I think you've proven the point, so I'll let you off the hook and find your dad and get him back on the dance floor." Janine motioned for them to make their way back to the table. "Mia's good for you," she said. "Don't let her slip away."

"I won't," he said, accepting her peck on the cheek. His last serious relationship before Mia had failed due to his missteps and tendency to put work first. He had no intention of making those same errors when it came to Mia—she'd his heart from day one; the day she made the effort to teach him the skills necessary to protect himself from the type of killers coming their way. She said he was the best weapon she had, because they wouldn't expect him to have any of the techniques she showed him. "And why does dad keep shutting you down?"

Janine gave a quick glance over her shoulder. "We want to talk to you about your work and honoring your brother's memory," she said, leading him off the dance floor. "And I need it to happen before we leave."

A knot formed in the pit of his belly as he kissed her cheek again. The tone of her voice signaled this was more than a simple request. His mother gave him a reassuring pat on the hand then slipped out of the ballroom.

The devil is coming . . .

Chapter 2

Calvin paused as the shadow of a man he could swear he saw earlier flickered into full view. One name came to mind—Gabriel London; the one man who could set Calvin's teeth on edge. The man who wouldn't be above using his parents trying to get to Calvin.

The devil is coming . . .

Before Calvin could give his mother's words, premonitions, or Gabriel London more thought, his phone pinged with a text message providing meeting details from Daron Kincaid, the owner of Crossroads Security. Mia had worked for him since they moved back to their new home, but Calvin also partnered with the enterprising inventor on projects at the Castle, an organization that was built for humanitarian purposes. Meeting? So soon? What the hell was going on?

Once Calvin found out about the unlimited resources the Castle had, and that the men who were now managing members were a dynamic group, he was hoping to become one of Daron's Knights. Then, not only would he be mentored by Daron himself, but eight other men who were former students of spiritual guru and philanthropist, Khalil Germaine. This mentoring program is where Calvin would not only learn from their specialized skills and extensive knowledge, but benefit from access to their global resources. It would solve some of his biggest career dilemmas; make sure his potential buyers were properly vetted, build global relationships, and that the end-user of the devices Calvin created were strictly to help people and communities that needed them most. This meeting, long before he had something to present, was not a good sign.

Calvin was approaching the table when he heard Mason ask, "Is everything all right?"

"Yes." Mia pressed her lips together into a forced grin, while casting a sorrowful gaze toward her clasped hands.

"I'm your father." Mason lifted her chin with an index finger. "I know when something isn't right."

Mia's eyes glazed over with tears. "I'm still reeling from Diana not being here anymore." She shrugged. "Sometimes it just catches me off guard. She loved to dance."

Calvin knew the unexpected death of Mia's friend had been difficult, but she seemed to be doing fine lately. He hadn't wanted to bring it up since grief was a delicate thing. Now looking at her with Mr. Jakob he wished he had.

"I'm here any time you need to talk." Mason pulled her into his massive chest.

Calvin slid into the chair next to Mia and waited until she lifted her head and said, "Hey, would you like to go home?"

"No, I'm good." Mia reached up to sweep her hair away from her face.

Mason grabbed his cell from the table. "Where are your parents?"

"Probably making their way back on the dance floor." Calvin glanced over the room and his gaze locked with a man whose attention was intently focused on the people at Calvin's table.

"Tell them it was nice seeing them again." Mason kissed Mia's forehead.

Mia's head snapped toward the crowd and her focus narrowed a bit. Mason's body tensed as he mimicked her actions.

"What?" Calvin asked hoping the two of them hadn't peeped something dangerous. He noticed his parents standing just outside the entrance talking to a tall, blond man in military fatigues. He shifted to her right, trying to see the man's face.

"I thought I saw an old friend from high school, but he moved out of the city." She scanned the crowd that had grown larger over the past half hour. "I can't imagine him not attending Diana's funeral if he was in town."

Mason frowned and barely contained his irritation. "Avant Arrington?"

She nodded as though saying more might be a problem.

Calvin had heard quite a few stories about her high school misadventures. "It would've been nice to meet the man you were always getting into trouble with."

"That's putting it mildly," Mason grumbled as he glanced at Mia, his left eyebrow winged upward. "It's probably for the best."

"Dad, Avant is a great person." Mia gave her father a reproachful gaze. "Why would you say that?"

Something in Mason's expression gave Calvin the impression that maybe there was more to their relationship than Avant being a "simple" part of her youthful crew as she claimed. He thought back to the feeling of something coming to turn his world upside down. At that moment, he was selfishly grateful that her high school "friend" was not there. Gabriel London. Avant Arrington.

The devil is already here. And he brought company.

Chapter 3

Mia entered the kitchen to see Calvin's handsome face hovering over a cup of coffee with his eyes closed, inhaling the scent of the roasted brew as if that medium ground roast was giving him life. His complexion was the color of Georgia pecans, her favorite thing to snack on during summers down South. The muscular body was the result of genetics and a rigorous daily routine that he'd kept up ever since she laid one out for him while they waited to take on seen and unseen enemies.

He opened his dark-brown eyes, took a sip, then gave her that lopsided first of the morning—I'm not quite right until that first cup of coffee—smile.

"Hey beautiful." Calvin handed her a cup, then rested his head against the Formica countertop of the island. "I'm feeling ooooooold. Can we call off and go back to bed?"

"Isn't that the reason you're worn out right now," she teased, setting the mug down and wrapping her arms around his waist. "Hey, at least it's Friday; you can push through."

"I'd rather be cuddled up with your fine self under the covers." Calvin pulled her in front of him, lowering his lips to hers.

"Snoring and—"

"Hey, I don't snore," he protested, narrowing his gaze on her.

"Oh, so that *was* an actual chainsaw letting loose in the backyard at three in the morning."

"You know what—"

"You do snore," she said. "But I notice it's when you're dog tired and used up all of your brain power for the day."

"I don't use all of my brain power on work," he confessed, cupping her face in his hands. "Some of it is used on my amazingly wonderful, brilliant woman."

"No, honey," she whispered. "I like to use up another part of your anatomy."

Mia kissed him and a rush of sensations enveloped her as he pressed his muscular body against her. Her body throbbed with desire, something that amazed her because her previous relationships didn't factor her pleasure into the equation. Calvin, a patient and thorough lover, always did. She gently pushed him back, knowing once they got started … "Don't tempt me."

Her gaze lowered to the wedding planner nestled between several cookbooks and binders.

Calvin kissed along her jaw, then down her neck before letting her slide away from him. "Have you seen my black folder with the blue strip?"

"It's probably in between the bed and dresser where you hid it when I came out of the shower." Mia chuckled, reclaiming her coffee, and looking at him over the rim of her *I Love Sexy Nerds* mug.

Calvin had come a long way, but dealing with the intricate levels and creativity that were required in his work was like breathing fresh air for him. Relaxing and enjoying life was the exact opposite. He was trying, though. She had to give him that much. Simple morning conversations were a huge accomplishment since he normally had his head into calculations and analysis the moment the ass crack of dawn spilt a little sun in the sky.

"Hiding something from you? Now would I do that?" Calvin gave her a sly grin that confirmed he believed that item was exactly where she said it was.

"Yes, you would." Her phone vibrated. She glanced at the notification to accept an incoming call from Daron as she told Calvin, "Work."

Her bare feet padded across the cool wooden floor leading to her office. Moments later a call came through and she tapped the talk button on the device that resembled a conference phone. The difference was that hers had the ability to project images.

"Morning." A hologram of Daron wearing a tailored black suit and his signature fedora appeared in the middle of the office. "Sorry for this last-minute call to change your assignment, but due to a family emergency we had to do some rearranging."

"Do I need to come into the office?" Mia opened the oak desk drawer, retrieved her gun and holster and slid them into place.

"You'll need to go straight to the location I just sent over." Daron pulled out the projector board on his end. "A woman witnessed a robbery and is being pressured by some local thugs who are threatening her daughter. The mother wants the little girl out of town for a couple of weeks. So she sent her to stay with the client."

"Is it the mother or the daughter who's in real danger?" Mia glanced at the downtown address. "Sounds like she needs to take precautions as well."

"There's a slight chance they're desperate enough to cross state lines to find the daughter to pressure the mother into staying quiet." Daron pulled the police file on the data board. "Separating them throws them off the trail. They suspect it wasn't just a simple robbery."

Mia slid the phone back into her pocket. "Is the mother up here?"

"She's in another location. Her daughter is with the client, who is a cousin, but he needs someone to protect her and the nanny while he works." Daron keyed a few words into the console and pulled up the image of a woman with alabaster skin, dark hair and features reminiscent of a runway model. "This is Emily, the nanny and the person you'll be meeting. I'm sending the file with full details."

"Has the nanny been checked out?" Mia wasn't thrilled about going into an assignment unprepared, but it happened occasionally.

"The client has utilized her services before. She arrived with the little girl, Toya, last night." Daron retrieved a picture of a young bright-eyed girl with the nanny. "You should have a moment to review and access what will be needed before she physically takes Toya out around nine."

"Good to know." Mia moved to a better vantage point to see the freshly planted garden from the office window.

"Emily won't be aware of the real reason you're there. The client just told her he wanted to ensure their safety, especially in an unfamiliar environment." Daron tapped the screen, closing the file. "If you leave now, you should make it on time."

Mia noticed a note at the top of Daron's board. *Follow up on police progress in forty-eight to seventy-two hours.*

Those words were never a good sign.

Chapter 4

Mia knocked on the door expecting the brunette she'd seen in the photos Daron showed her earlier. Instead, a handsome bearded man with grayish-blue eyes who stood just over six feet tall opened the door. He wore a short-sleeve crisp white dress shirt that accentuated a chiseled chest that men were nearly killing themselves to achieve.

"What are you doing here?" Mia had not expected a familiar face when she arrived at this new assignment.

"I didn't realize you were in the protection field." Avant stepped forward hugging her close before she could protest that he shouldn't. "I would've thought you'd be DEA, FBI, CIA or something."

"And I thought I'd be meeting Emily." She stepped into a modestly furnished contemporary townhome, the scent of citrus warred with a hint of garlic which meant they'd either eaten a meal recently or another was about to be served.

"You were, but my meeting was pushed back." Avant closed the door. "I thought I'd wait and meet the person watching over Toya."

"Are you going to walk me through the place or should I have Emily do it?" Mia attempted to keep things strictly business. Memories of their youthful antics filled her mind. None of them would be deemed anywhere close to professional.

"I'd love to show you around," he said, leading her back into the living room. "It's fairly small. Three bedrooms and an office upstairs."

"How's the rest of the family?" Mia asked, taking in the exposed wood beams in the ceiling, refusing to meet his intense eyes head on. She could practically feel the heat of his gaze on her and refused to make eye contact.

"Good." He guided her to where the double concrete islands separated the living room from the kitchen.

"Is your little brother still leaving a trail of broken hearts?" Mia asked, following him down the hallway past a home gym as he pointed out the main floor bathroom.

"Unfortunately, yes." Avant chuckled as they headed upstairs where he gestured to the bedrooms, office, and second level bathroom. The place would be easy to secure. At least a lot more so than her last assignment—Calvin Atwood. His place in the suburbs was a virtual nightmare of proxemics with a lake and wooded area in the rear, and a restaurant district nearly a half block away. The combination alone allowed access for their enemies to come far too close to their intended target.

Mia and Avant made their way back downstairs. "How long have you been in town?"

"I arrived a couple of weeks before Diana's funeral." He pulled out his cell, glancing at the display.

She placed her bag in an oversized beige chair. "I'm surprised I didn't see you there."

"I was late and ended up in the overflow room." Avant slid his hands into his pocket and leaned against the couch. "I saw you, but I couldn't get through the crowd to speak to you. You weren't at the repast."

"I had to work." Mia pulled a tablet from her bag. She couldn't believe how his boyish good looks had matured into this GQ model. The man was the direct opposite of Calvin's intense ruggedness that housed a brain so brilliant, she marveled at his inventions and his ability to explain the use of them in such a way that she didn't feel deficient.

"I still can't believe she's gone." Avant stood and his solemn tone forced her to look his way.

"Yeah." His eyes reflected the sadness and loss that existed in her heart. "I thought we had time to make more memories."

Avant's gaze bored into hers. "Remember how she'd bring us those deluxe lunches because we were always doing something other than eating during our meal period?" He crossed his arms, causing the shirt to stretch over his chest.

Mia tore her eyes away from his pecs and put her attention on analyzing the file Daron sent her. "Until you got busted eating it in class."

"Hey, I can't find my gym bag." A beautiful girl with a sienna complexion and small afro ran toward them.

"Didn't you put it in the foyer last night?" He smiled, glancing at his watch as she took off toward the door. "That little blur of human was Toya, by the way."

"She's a cutie pie."

Toya grabbed a bright pink bag and raced back up the stairs.

"I don't know what my cousin was thinking. A single man with no children to watch over her ten-year-old daughter for two weeks." Avant stroked his neatly trimmed beard. "Man, Emily has been saving my clueless behind, but we definitely have to work on her manners."

Mia stared at him while he popped his fingers at the first sentence. Definitely one of the "tells" when he was exaggerating. "How long before you leave out?"

"Thirty minutes."

"Since you're here, I'm going to do an assessment of the outside and surrounding area to make sure they're secure." Before he could say anything more, she went to her car and reviewed the file.

They attempted to take Toya while she was playing in the park with some friends. Broad daylight. Bold. Real bold. Daron noted that something was off about the case. If Mia noticed anyone following them, she was supposed to let the team know and they'd dig into things a little more. She placed the tablet back into the tote bag and noticed Calvin had stashed a red box with a gold ribbon emblem on it. Mia pulled out the box which turned out to be her favorite chocolates, but she only treated herself to them on rare occasions. The note said *a little something special for someone who's exquisite.*

She couldn't help the smile that lifted the corners of her lips as she dialed Calvin.

"Hey, is everything okay?" Calvin's voice was filled with concern. Understandable because she rarely called in the mornings, since they hit the ground running. Like today.

"No. I found that little special something you slipped in my bag. Thanks." She resisted the urge to open the box. "I may need it to keep up with the bundle of energy I'm guarding."

"You're welcome," he said, and his voice was husky with the promise of things to come. "You know I adore you."

Mia scanned the area, taking in the well-manicured landscape of the housing on the tree-lined street. "I've got to get back to it. See you tonight. Love you."

"I love you more."

"No, you love me also," she said beginning that age-old debate they had from time to time.

She exited the car, bypassed the house and continued along the pathway leading in the opposite direction from how she arrived. Mia paid close attention to the homes that had direct sightlines to Avant's place and mentally noted her concerns. She retraced her steps to the car, then grabbed the bag that had more appropriate clothes for guarding a child.

Avant was waiting near the door when she came back inside and formally introduced her to Emily and Toya.

Emily gave her a disdainful once over, frowned as she flickered a gaze between Avant and Mia as though the gender and size difference mattered for some reason. Mia didn't bother to advise her of the fact that her qualifications were more suited to the job than Avant.

After Emily helped Toya finish her studies, Mia joined them for a few rounds of Jenga, Memory, and Uno, until it was time to leave. Emily locked up as they headed out to take Toya to her regularly scheduled activities. Though Mia advised against doing such a thing, the mother insisted they keep to the normal routine for Toya's sake. Mia expected the day to drag, but time flew by. Toya's excitement was contagious as she talked nonstop about swimming at the YMCA and visiting the Museum of Science and Industry on the way back to the townhouse. She had Mia and Emily in stitches with her stories.

Watching Toya made Mia realize that she had kept pushing marriage and children to the back burner for far too long. She never seemed to have the right balance of everything in a relationship to actually put things in motion. Since Calvin had slowed down, having children had been on her mind a lot recently. Spending time with Toya just fortified the desire to have kids. She needed to nail down the wedding date as Calvin had been hedging for a hot minute. Well, his parents, mostly.

An hour after returning to the townhouse, a key struggling to make it into the lock snapped Mia to attention. Everyone who mattered was already in the house. She hopped up and sprinted to the door.

Avant entered, froze, dropped the packages in his arms, then held up both hands.

Mia let out a long slow breath and slipped her gun back into the holster. "Don't do that. I could have shot you."

"I'm sorry. I wasn't thinking." Avant shook his head and put a wary glance on her gun before he scooped up the packages and placed them on the foyer table. "I'm working from home for the remainder of the day. If you need me, I'll be in my office."

Mia almost felt her presence wasn't needed if he was going to be around. Two hours later, it seemed Avant was officially off the clock. Emily, Mia, Toya, and Avant had elevated to Phase Ten and Monopoly in the living room for the next few hours.

"Emily, can you get Toya ready for bed now?" Avant asked after the little minx had maneuvered into staying up a little past her bedtime.

Toya pouted, looking every bit of her ten years. "It's too early."

"Your mom wants to do a video chat." Avant put up the cards. "If you get ready for bed now, we won't have to rush off so that Emily can give you a bath before she leaves for the day."

"Okay." That pout remained in place as she followed Emily upstairs.

"For a man who doesn't have kids, you're really comfortable with her." Mia pushed off the wood floor and moved to the couch.

"Well, Toya and her mom have stayed with me for several short stints over the years." Avant placed the cards on the coffee table and joined Mia on the couch. "I love my cousin but she's the worst judge of character. You can't tell Leticia anything. She'd been doing good these couple of years, until this incident."

"I assume Emily used to help during those times." He nodded as her phone vibrated, letting her know the shift was officially over. It made sense the photo in the file with Emily was when Toya was younger. "It's really great seeing you."

He shifted to face her on the couch. "I hate that I lost touch."

"What happened?" Mia gathered her things and stood, keeping some distance between them.

"I got a little lost my first semester in college, got a girl knocked up."

Mia tilted her head. Avant being a father was not something she pictured.

"No, nothing like that. She lost the baby." He stood as she slung her bag onto her shoulder. "My entire life got derailed. I felt embarrassed. The boy voted most likely to succeed had screwed up his life straight out the gate."

Mia moved toward the door. "You seem to have pulled it together." She peered out of the window and noticed someone watching the house. Too late for it to be a casual visitor for the neighbors. She made a mental note to get the plate numbers.

"Yeah, it took me a minute." He leaned on the wall next to the door, crossing his arms over his chest as he narrowed a gaze on her. "But I went in with a plan and messed it up."

Mia nodded, stepped out on the stone porch unprepared for what Avant would say next.

"You were my best friend."

She glanced over her shoulder to find the softness in his eyes matched that of his voice.

"I always intended to come back for you."

Mia didn't know how to respond. Instead, she smiled and gave it a moment's thought before saying, "I meant to do better at keeping in touch. I need to go. See you tomorrow."

Her mind was reeling from Avant's comment. She convinced herself that he didn't mean it like it sounded. At least, she hoped he didn't.

She headed to her car at a measured pace, taking note of the dark sedan's plates and the fact that she was too far away to get a good look at the driver.

Who the hell was casing the house?

Chapter 5

"What are you doing here?" Calvin stared at the blond stocky man who was sitting across from his parents having drinks and appetizers. His crew cut was as tight and severe as his attitude.

"Don't be rude." His mom swatted his hand as if he was still a child. He was glad Mia was running late. She would not be happy with his parents right now.

Calvin had walked straight into his favorite lunch joint and right into an ambush. Janine and Bruce had been disappointed when they found out that his most daring invention to date had not been commissioned for Gabriel London's team to use. At the Stepper's Set, his mother mentioned that they wanted to discuss something important with him, but he hadn't expected them to invite Gabriel London to lunch.

"Gabriel was telling us a bit about the project that he wanted you to consult on." Bruce nodded toward the man to his right.

"We heard your Emperor's Suit is currently in an exclusive contract with some other organization, which was disappointing." Gabriel shifted in his chair. His long limbs stretched into the aisle in such a way to inconvenience anyone trying to walk past.

The devil seems to have a name. Gabriel London.

Calvin could feel the money lust rolling off the man like an overflowing washbasin. The one thing he learned the hard way was that people tended to play both sides of the fence. Some for money, others for what they believed to be a higher calling. Some days he had to admit that those lucrative offers made him want to accept them at face value. Then after the ordeal that brought Mia into his life, he realized the lengths to which greed would drive people.

Now that he was in line with Daron and The Kings of the Castle, he didn't have to wonder about motives. This meant that Calvin could maintain his purpose, which was to help people and not profit off their pain. Enough people in the world were doing just that.

"He wanted an opportunity to speak more about having you consult on a new project that would help your brother's old team," Janine explained smiling, totally oblivious of the things she was putting into play.

Calvin frowned at his parents as Gabriel's gaze shifted to a table close to them where two men sat who seemed totally out of place for such a casual eatery. "And I thought you two wanted to spend time with your son."

This was not how he expected an enjoyable Saturday afternoon to go. They could have at least given him a heads up. But then again, they knew how he felt about Gabriel, so they knew not mentioning him was the best way to ensure he'd show up.

"We do, but we also know you may have lost focus on the goal of creating devices to help people like your brother," Bruce countered, popping a slider into his mouth. "Ones that would increase the number of them that come home."

"I'm sorry that I was so optimistic when I said that, not thinking about who could be in power and in control of my device." Calvin watched as Gabriel silently took in the exchange between them. "I'm no longer confident that the American government is out to use it to change the world."

"I beg to differ," Gabriel said, waving off the red-haired waitress as she approached then had to adjust because he wouldn't shift to accommodate the fact she needed to get past. His parents would have chided him up one side of the earth and rattled his cage down the other if he had done something so inconsiderate. Why couldn't they see the real Gabriel.

"You would." Calvin didn't miss that Gabriel had his parents doing most of the talking. Possibly believing that they would sway him. He was wrong.

"Calvin, at least hear him out," Janine pleaded.

"We have a product that could be beneficial to soldiers, but we're having trouble with certain aspects of the design." Gabriel's phone rang. He silenced it without checking the screen. "Your experience could be essential to making this a reality."

"What is the product?" Calvin noticed Gabriel had no paperwork with him, so this discussion was slated to end in a continuance of some sort.

"Unfortunately, that can't be revealed until you're contracted as a consultant," Gabriel answered. His smile was alarming, because it was insincere.

"That's not going to work, I need to know what it is before I dive-in. You put me under contract for one thing, and suddenly the scope changes and I'm on the hook for doing something else entirely." Calvin glanced in the direction that Gabriel's eyes kept straying. A table full of men who appeared to be military. Maybe they were listening in somehow.

Gabriel tossed the rest of his drink down and placed the tumbler on the table. "I'll have a confidentiality agreement drawn up so that we can further discuss it."

"It's a start." Calvin noticed his parents sharing a knowing glance and wondered how long Gabriel had been there talking with them before he'd arrived. Either way, he wanted him gone before Mia arrived. She would pick up on the nuances that his parents certainly hadn't.

"I'll let you enjoy your lunch. We can arrange another time when the paperwork is in place." Gabriel stood, shaking hands with Bruce and Janine. "Thanks. I'll be in touch."

A few minutes later, the men at the table across from them left the restaurant. Calvin didn't miss that Gabriel hadn't bothered to exchange any information with either of his parents—his entire conversation was directed towards Calvin.

"Mom and Dad, I love you, but you cannot do things like this." Calvin tried to keep the anger out of his voice. "You don't understand how dangerous some of these people are."

"We've known Gabriel since your brother enlisted," Janine huffed, her gaze sharp and as intense as her voice had been.

"You don't know if fighting has changed him," Calvin said, leveling a hard look her way. "Shawn is no longer here to keep us informed."

Calvin needed his parents to understand the importance of letting this go. His trust level for the government and for the military was at an all-time low. Instead of waiting for him to complete that first project, they sent in a team to kill him and take it. Then they would own it and wouldn't have to pay him the millions they promised. Soon, Mia was fending off foreign and domestic enemies until Calvin could put the device in the hands of the right people. The fact that Gabriel was here saying he represented the very same government that Calvin swore never to work for again, spoke volumes.

"We've stayed in touch," Janine admitted, and those words were startling. How much had they told Gabriel about his line of work? How much ammunition had they given him? His parents were patriots through and through, and Calvin never wanted to disillusion them by sharing the facts behind his near brush with death.

A large group came near and were seated after the waiters put several tables together.

"Did you forget why the Emperor's Suit didn't end up being used by soldiers." Calvin still didn't want to get into the full details on the attempt to steal the device that led him to decide against giving it to the government. The first good thing that came out of it is his relationship with Mia. The second good thing is that he could no longer work with the understanding that even his own government would play fair. Good and evil existed in all factions of life, but he would be damned if he didn't figure out where he, and his inventions, fit into the scheme of things. The third good thing was a renewed sense of purpose.

"We didn't forget, but we don't want you to completely rule out the possibility." Bruce took Janine's hand in his and she gave him a look so filled with love that it made Calvin smile.

"Why is this so important to you?" Calvin asked after giving them a moment.

Janine leaned toward him, trying to make sure her voice was heard over the hum of conversation. "It would keep your brother's memory alive, and help the men he cared so much about."

"We do that by not allowing monsters to abuse and profit off a device meant to protect people who are willing to put their lives at risk to help others." He glanced up in time to see Mia enter and weave her way through the aisles of wooden tables. She wore a simple pink blouse and black slacks, but even the way those fit on her was sexy—understated elegance. Those heels, though. Killer. Work was definitely going to take a back seat today. They were going to have an impromptu date with a yacht trip on Lake Michigan. She would love that.

Calvin stood, pulling out Mia's seat and kissing her before she lowered herself into the chair. "Hey beautiful," he whispered so only she could hear.

"I'm sorry I'm late." Mia put her eyes on Calvin, staring for a moment, as if she could feel the tension in the air. "Traffic was terrible."

"You're right on time." Calvin handed her a menu and tapped on the blueberry pancakes which happened to be a favorite.

"Yes, because now we can talk about why you two aren't married already." Janine reached into the oversized tote hanging on the back of her chair and pulled out several wedding books and dropped them dramatically on the table.

Janine Atwood was swinging for the fences today. As if inviting Gabriel here wasn't enough. "Really, Mom?" Calvin stared at his mother, while ignoring his father's attempt at stifling a laugh. She had been pushy, but never this adamant. "Is this what we're doing today?"

"I'm ready for grandchildren," Janine protested, pinning him with a look that said *That issue with Gordon was out of my wheelhouse. But this right here ... no, my brother, I'm not going to drop this one.* "If Mia can get you to slow down enough to dance, I realized that you might actually slow down enough to become a father."

Even Mia flinched at that one. "Mrs. Atwood, I tried for us to get married at City Hall, since his schedule didn't seem to allow us to nail down the date, but he is *insisting* on a full wedding." Mia turned and smiled at him sweetly.

Calvin couldn't believe his future wife would throw him into the lion's den with a rare steak nailed to his forehead! What the hell was going on today?

Maybe this was her way of getting back at him for working late last night and leaving out too early to say a proper good morning. He refrained from reminding Mia that *they* had selected a date. Diana's unexpected death was the reason Mia couldn't finalize the contract on the space. With her maid of honor gone, celebrating their union was the last thing on her mind. "Am I wrong to want to see my beautiful bride being walked down the aisle by her father? Who, by the way, is only too happy to do so."

"No, but sometimes you have to amend your vision to fit your reality," Bruce fired back, passing Calvin a copy of *Brides Noir*. "While we'd love to celebrate your love with a fancy wedding and all that, the most important thing is for you and Mia to officially become a family."

"Your father's right," Janine co-signed, but her tone said otherwise.

Calvin was glad to see the waitress approaching the table. He hadn't been expecting that response, especially from his mother, who had, for all her earlier protestations that year, been looking forward to wedding preparations and every ounce of fanfare. This was an entire one-eighty.

Janine pulled out a calendar. "Let's pick a date."

"Mom, Enough," Calvin warned, causing the waitress to freeze, then swivel in the direction of another table. "No more harassing us about wedding date. We'll get married. You'll be invited, and that's that."

His mom's jaw dropped and her eyes widened. He was done coddling his parents. First that whole push with Gabriel, then the wedding issue. His life, and he wanted them to be a part of things, but they were not going to dictate things this way.

"Calvin has to go back to work after this, but maybe I can take the two of you to our top three venues." Mia placed a hand on Calvin's thigh; a subtle move that was supposed to reassure him that she had everything under control. She didn't know Janine Atwood well enough to realize that control was lost the moment she walked through the door. But Mia was a woman who could handle her business, and he didn't need to fight her battles. "They probably have events going on so we may only be able to peek in."

"I'd love that," Janine exclaimed, her smile firmly back in place but with a quick stink eye at Calvin.

The rest of the lunch was more relaxed, with them talking about some of the family members his parents had visited on Friday. He listened, but his thoughts panned to Gabriel once again, wondering what his second attack would be. Parents were the first line to sink in a hook. Men like Gabriel did not give up.

He thought the remainder of the day would be smooth sailing. Little did he know that the ambush meeting with Gabriel was already causing ripples that would build to a tidal wave.

Chapter 6

Calvin drove through the wooded grounds toward The Castle property, a place situated on acres of sprawling greenery with everything from horse stables, several swimming pools, basketball and tennis courts, to a lake and an eighteen-hole golf course. He glanced upward at the stone tower and was grateful for the change in his life that this opportunity had given him. Nine men from different areas of Chicago, all professionals, had been called forth to further a vision of a man who understood the reality of life, but still embraced hope and did his part to bring people of the world together. Finally realizing that people like these men existed, gave flight to Calvin's purpose.

He entered the main building, heading to the Morgan Park wing where the lab was housed.

When he swiped into the secured door, Daron, the King of Morgan Park, was the first person he laid eyes on. The steely gaze he lasered on Calvin was unnerving, but then again, Daron always had an intense air about him.

What could've happened within the few hours since I stepped away?

Daron motioned for Calvin to follow him.

He glanced into the lab through the glass wall on one side of the hallway before entering Daron's private office. Calvin settled in a black executive chair in front of a mahogany desk.

"Do we need to reevaluate this partnership?" Daron propped up on his elbows.

"I don't think so." Calvin wondered what prompted that question, but he was leery of asking. After lunch with his parents, he certainly didn't want to deal with any more drama.

"Why were you meeting with Gabriel London?" Daron turned the tablet around showing a photo taken in the restaurant earlier. "Are you working on a project with him?"

Calvin couldn't believe one brief unexpected conversation would lead to this. "I have not agreed to consult on any project with Gabriel. Are you all tailing me?"

Daron was silent for a moment, as though weighing how much to share. "We're tailing Gabriel. He is under surveillance for suspicious activity. Not only in the United States but also overseas." He slid the device back and rested it on his thigh. "The problem is that rumors are floating around that you're working on something in the field of chemical warfare."

"How would anyone even know that?" Calvin leaned back in the chair, pondering that information for a moment. "I haven't mentioned that to anyone."

"People are paying attention to the seminars you're attending and the items you have on order." Daron flipped the tablet's screen toward Calvin displaying the compilation of pictures from events he recently participated in. "I've been waiting for you to bring your concept to the table, hoping that you're not developing weapons of mass destruction."

"Of course I'm not," Calvin protested, unnerved that even when he had taken himself off the radar, someone was monitoring him much too closely. "I'm developing more of a personal protective against an attack."

Daron's body language was taut and made Calvin uneasy. "I'm assuming this is something you're trying to weave into the Emperor's Suit or at least alongside of it."

"Yes." Calvin shifted in the chair, feeling more like he was under interrogation.

Daron moved to his computer. "You're one of nine men in line to become a Knight and work with me to fulfill my purpose at the Castle. You can't keep things of this magnitude to yourself," he said, his nimble fingers flying over the keys. "Not only do you make yourself a target, but me and my brother kings as well."

"I'm accustomed to getting to the point where I at least have a working prototype before I present ideas." Calvin hoped he hadn't ruined his one shot at being a Knight. The Castle was the one place Calvin was sure didn't have the same kind of motives that drove the American government or its enemies. "I'll keep it in mind for the future."

"Well, Khalil and I would like to have a talk about your future with us." Daron nodded for Calvin to follow him.

Calvin's worry now outpaced his anger as he trailed Daron through the maze of corridors in the Castle to the state-of-the-art command center where all the Kings and Khalil were present. Some were physically there, others via hologram conferencing. Several semi-circular conference tables ringed the room, each table on its own level of flooring, becoming slightly bigger than the one below it. A few of the Kings were sitting at the conference table at the bottom facing the wall of LCD screens.

"You can sit here." Daron pointed to the second-tier right above the Kings.

Khalil Germaine's deep-olive skin and shiny black hair with a sliver of grey at the widow's peak appeared as a hologram in the center of where the Kings were seated. He turned in Calvin's direction. "We are committed to addressing the inhumane issues going on in this world, and I believe you can be an integral part of that."

Dro Reyes, the King of Hyde Park, peered at him a moment. He was tall, about the same height as Daron and several of the other men at the table, but he had a complexion that reflected his Latino heritage. "You could have accepted the offer that would have put billions in your bank account, but you didn't, and that speaks volumes," Dro said.

Daron took a black and gold letter size folder from Vikkas, the King of Wilmette.

"I'm all for making a profit, but my main goal is to protect those who risk their lives for others." Calvin kept his eyes focused on Khalil's and not the others whose intense stares threatened to drill holes right through him.

"We have a proposal for you. We want you to become a Knight," Daron stated, handing him the folder that had the letters Knight of South Holland engraved on the front.

"I would love the opportunity."

"The first project would be development of a system to protect Durabia," Khalil said.

"Durabia," Calvin repeated slightly surprised. Durabia was a country in the Middle East located near the Arabian gulf, a growing metropolis without a prominent military force. The United States had a good relationship with Durabia. They were peaceful people who left the wars to other countries in that area. Why would they need such protection now?

"Is there a problem?" Shaz, the King of Evanston, asked, grabbing a sandwich and bottled water from the food station along the sidewall. His waist-length locs and appetite were both legendary.

"I just need a little more clarity on what I'm attempting to shield them from." Calvin was excited to create a system to protect people. He hadn't expected a global project straight out the gate. All the more reason to distance himself from Gabriel and his parents' demands.

"A protective military shield from chemical warfare would be our first initiative," Khalil answered.

Daron shot him a look as if to say *you should have been able to guess that one*.

"Let me remind you that you signed a confidentiality clause and that you recognize what happens in The Castle stays in The Castle," Vikkas added as Jai, the King of Devon, turned the page on a document he'd been studying since Calvin walked in.

"Mia has been a vital part of brainstorming on the project." Calvin glanced down at the contents of the folder Daron had given him. His mind was already spinning and creating ways to alter products the two of them had already developed to fit this project. Mia, who had a wonderful way of balancing Calvin's concepts when he needed to brainstorm, would be a welcome partner in some of his newer inventions. She grasped things about his work that people who had been in the industry for years couldn't seem to understand. That's one of the reasons he added her name to every single invention and patent in which she gave input. If something happened to him, then the work would live on through her, and she would receive financial benefits for the rest of her life.

"Yes, since you would need to move there temporarily, maybe for one to three years," Khalil answered. "And she's already been cleared by Dro."

Calvin's head whipped to Khalil. "Dro? But she already—"

"Yes, though she works for Daron," Khalil said, leveling a gaze on him. "It would be a conflict of interest, if we didn't have a neutral person to run point."

"Majority of the work can be done stateside," Calvin said, trying to remain focused on the conversation instead of jotting down the ideas flooding his brain. "Setup and final testing would understandably require my presence."

"Kamran Ali Khan will be available to answer any questions you have on Durabia," Khalil stated before wrapping up the meeting and letting the Kings disperse.

"Just know we will meet with some resistance to the project," Daron added, placing a schedule in front of Calvin.

Calvin reviewed the document and one thing stood out more than all the others. "Weapons training."

"Every morning before you start work." Daron escorted Calvin to the exit. "I'll be increasing your protection detail, but you'll also be trained to take care of yourself. Mia can't be everywhere at once."

Chapter 7

Mia agreed to a crack of dawn breakfast meeting at Original Pancake House with her dad to ease his concerns about what she'd said about Diana the other night. While she didn't want her father to worry about her, she was worried about Calvin. He'd been acting weird ever since Saturday and was, sadly, back in workaholic mode for some reason. Mia suspected that he was intentionally trying to avoid having a conversation about his parents. She also wanted to question him about that group of military men congregrating outside the restaurant. One of them, a blond muscular man, seemed to eye her with great interest.

"Do you still like your job?" Mason's question drew her attention back to the conversation.

"Working with Daron at Crossroads has been a blessing and an adventure." Mia sipped the dark roast brew. She wasn't ready to talk about how she was actually reevaluating her career path. She always wanted to have kids but she hadn't considered the impact her job could have on them until recently. "I've actually been guarding Avant's cousin, Toya."

Mason scowled at the mention of Avant. "You might want to make it clear that you're not available. If history serves as a reminder, he's looking to reconnect as more than a friend."

When they had shipped her to a private high school outside their neighborhood, she'd thought her life was over. Then she met Avant and Diana, and it was the beginning of some of the most memorable years of her life. The two of them helped her through some of the most difficult times.

"It's not like that." Mia shifted the cup on the table, no longer interested in the warmth the coffee would provide.

Mason raised a bushy eyebrow. "Then why do I feel like that time I caught you sneaking home in the morning after spending all night with him."

Mia had lied that night and said she had only been out with Diana. The master interrogator finally got the truth out of her. Switching subjects was the best plan of attack, because this was one discussion she did not want to have. Her mind flashed back to Avant's statement. *Surely, he hadn't meant it that way.*

"Other things are going on. Calvin's parents are unknowingly placing him in danger."

Mason shifted his chair forward, leaning in toward her. "How?"

She scanned the people around them, but the quaint diner only had a few customers at this early hour. "By pressuring him to do business with a man who served with his brother."

"But you think he's up to no good."

"I feel it deep in my soul that Gabriel London is working with someone who wants Calvin's inventions for their own deviant purpose." Mia sliced through her blueberry pancakes that had been lathered in butter with only a few drops of syrup. "To be honest, I'm still not sure he wasn't one of the teams involved in the first attempt to steal the Emperor's Suit."

"Honey, because of who Calvin is and what he does, he'll always be dealing with someone who's duplicitous, straddles the fence and plays both sides." He laid his hand over hers. "The long engagement? Are you having doubts if you can handle that for the rest of your life?"

Mia twisted her engagement ring between her fingers. "I'm more concerned that death will do us part before we achieve our dream of having a family."

* * *

Four hours later, Mia found herself at a waterpark with not only the nanny and two young girls, but Avant in tow. Clearly, his definition of working remotely was drastically different from hers. Emily, who was wearing a body-gripping lime one-piece with a sheer center, seemed pleased with this new development. Mia lost count of how many times Emily had managed to touch Avant while playing in the water with the girls.

Her focus was on a woman standing among the people who were watching Toya and Avant. Mia instantly went on high alert. She pulled the camera from a bag next to her, then pretended to take some pictures of the girls. She sent the images off to the team and waited for them to get back to her. Something told her to also send the picture off to Cameron Stone, Daron's mate and a fellow security specialist.

An hour later Avant emerged from the pool and several women put their focus on him. "The girls seem to be having a blast."

"They are." Mia set her phone aside for a moment, though the information she wanted hadn't come in.

Avant slid the towel over his sculpted chest, sopping up the water. He checked his cell, oblivious to the attention on him. Mia still couldn't believe her rail-thin friend was buff and sexy now.

He grabbed his wallet. "Do you want anything?"

"Something to drink," Mia replied, still keeping an eye on the woman to make sure she wasn't a factor.

Toya ran over, blocking her view. "Emily told me to let you know we're going to the other side."

"Okay, but walk—don't run—back to her." Avant lowered himself into the chair while watching Toya.

"Your daughter is too cute," a petite woman with dark brown skin and box braids said, smiling as a young boy dragged her past them.

Avant's eyes went wide, apparently too shocked to correct her. "Um, thank you?"

Mia couldn't speak. The woman's resemblance to their late friend had thrown her too. The big brown eyes, the button nose, and heart-shaped lips were so much like Diana it was like a punch to the gut.

His head swiveled toward her. "Was it just me or did she look like …."

"If it wasn't for her height, they could've been twins." Mia stared at the petite woman sliding into the pool with her son. "I'm still in shock. Her death was so senseless."

Avant slid his shirt on then grabbed hold of her hand. "I couldn't believe it when I heard."

"When did men become so fragile?" Mia still couldn't digest that her friend had been killed for turning down a man's advances. She was already engaged to be married. Of course, "no" was the logical answer to anyone else who wanted to pursue any type of relationship with her. Who knew that simple word could trigger a man to put a bullet in a woman he'd never met before? "It's becoming more of an epidemic."

Avant gently caressed her hand. "Studying men with that level of mental instability may be the only way to identify why. Then counseling before they reach that point."

"You're probably right, but I only see a monster." Mia slipped her hand from his, thinking about what her father had said earlier about feeling that Avant might try to come between her and Calvin. She would not let that happen. "I don't always think about what created them or if there are ways to keep them from going down that path."

"You can't teach a young lady how to protect herself from that kind of madness. That's the scariest thing of all." Avant's phone beeped. This time, he took a glance at the screen and frowned.

"Rejection isn't easy for anyone, but killing someone over it is extreme." Mia put eyes on the girls who were barreling down the slide at top speed.

"When you rejected me in high school, I was hurt, but I never thought *take her out*."

"I didn't reject you." Mia popped him hard on his bicep. "You never expressed an interest outside of friendship."

"Oh, I was interested, but I do remember Miss Mia Jakob frowning up her face and squawking every time someone mentioned we were a cute couple. Then she took a pointed interest in reminding them we were just friends." Avant grimaced the same way she did every time someone asked if they were "together".

"We were *only* friends which means I didn't reject you."

"You vetoed the idea of us being a couple like it was a skin-eating disease, thereby rejecting me as a possible mate." He grabbed her hand with the engagement ring. "I can't lie. Now that we've reconnected, I hate that you're with this guy. I wanted it to be me." Avant's phone vibrated. "I need to take this."

Mia stared at Avant as he stepped away to take what she could only assume was a business call. She couldn't believe she hadn't known his feelings back then. The mystery lady shifted position, suddenly moving in the direction Avant had gone.

"Sorry, work emergency," Avant said when he returned several moments later and handed her a bottle of water. He slid his phone back into his bag.

"Hold down our spot." Mia stood, sliding the tote over her shoulder. "I'll be right back"

Mia took a chance that the woman would continue any surveillance efforts. She aimed for the exit to run to the room that Avant had rented in case he needed to step away to work. Then she could grab the ghost drone from among the rest of her gear. She was surprised when Cameron Stone stepped on the elevator along with her. Cameron was a colorful character. She used to live a double life, one expertly breaking the same laws the men in her family were sworn to uphold and protect. The other as a respected entrepreneur with almost as many degrees as she had businesses. While Mia and Cameron were becoming great friends, there was so much mystery in her past that often Mia didn't know what was fact or fiction.

An elderly couple stepped towards the elevator, but Cameron, wearing a nondescript outfit that blended quite well with the hotel's clientele, headed them off by sliding toward Mia and pulling her into an embrace, saying in a seductive voice, "Haven't seen you since this morning. We need to make up for lost time."

Mia blinked several times before she caught on and turned to the couple, "Hope you're not uncomfortable with PDAs."

"What?" the silver-haired man said, his puzzled expression landing on his wife who answered, "Public displays of affection. We'll take the next one."

"Wait, I'd like to watch," he said, and his wife elbowed him in the side so hard that he doubled over in pain.

As the elevator doors closed, Mia chuckled as she said, "You are so wrong for that."

"She shouldn't be a danger to you or Toya." Cameron leaned on the wood paneling.

"So you know her?"

"Her name is Tyler," Cameron said, moving closer to the silver doors. "She's a detective who saw her best friend murdered a few years back. Our paths have crossed, but she knows me under another alias."

"Why do you think she's here?" Mia stepped off the elevator and headed to the room.

"Looking into Avant." Cameron pulled out a tablet.

Mia opened the door, letting Cameron in first. "Why Avant?"

"Because the company he works for assigns him at random." Cameron handed her the tablet. "But I get the feeling it's like not everyone he's consulting for is above board."

"What makes you say that?"

"I'm not saying he's intentionally working with criminals." She perched on the arm of the couch. "I'm saying he's probably given enough information to make an informed decision, but not enough to realize there's a problem. Until there is one."

"Damn, maybe I should talk to him about it." Mia angled to move past her and make it back outside before Avant came looking for her. Cameron grabbed Mia's arm to hold her in place.

"Stay out of it." Cameron released her arm. "Tyler may be working with her boyfriend, whose job falls into the government's grey area. There's a rumor a group hires unsuspecting people to manage their company's illegal project. Innocent people have died or been sent to prison."

"Considering what Calvin does, I definitely don't need to bring attention to him." She glanced down at the information on the screen. "But if Avant's in trouble ..."

Cameron gave her a once over. "Is there something going on between you and Avant? Because you know how this works."

"No, he's just a good friend," Mia said, placing the tablet back in Cameron's hands.

Cameron gave her a look that translated into *stop lying*, then returned the device to her jacket. "A good enough friend that you're willing to risk your fiancé's life and safety by jumping to conclusions and not doing your due diligence."

"It's not like that," Mia denied, but felt a little chagrined that she would point out something like this.

"It isn't? Because you looked like you were two seconds from running over to question him like a rookie." Cameron stood, zipping up her jacket. "Merely on rumors and suspicions instead of discreetly investigating like a pro."

Mia closed her eyes, instantly chastised and filtered through everything that had been said for the past few minutes. "I just don't understand why Tyler's here. This isn't exactly an office environment."

"Look, it's not any of my business." Cameron lifted her shoulders in a casual shrug. "All I'm going to say is you might need to take some time for yourself. You're off your game and that could get a lot of people in trouble."

"I'm fine." Her standard answer, even though Cameron's words were vibrating through her entire being. *You're off your game and that could get a lot of people in trouble.*

"Maybe even see a grief counselor." Cameron stared down at her. "Death affects people differently, and it's okay not to be all right."

"I hear you, Dr. Stone." Mia was disturbed by the information she had read. She could understand why it was a delicate situation.

"Maybe approach Tyler instead of questioning Avant." Cameron scanned the two-bedroom suite, and Mia could practically see her calculating the truth behind the earlier assertion that nothing was going on. "At least you'll know what to discreetly ask him to find out what's going on."

Mia decided with the new information she didn't need the drone after all. "Thanks."

"It could be that he's looking suspicious because he changed his routine to spend more time with you."

Cameron winked, then slipped out of the room before Mia could reply.

Chapter 8

The anger that flared in Mia's eyes made Calvin wish he had delayed the conversation until later. The bedroom walls were doing a nasty tango in the wrong direction towards closing in on him. In truth, he should have had a discussion with her earlier.

"You're determined to get yourself killed?" Mia softly bit her lip then looked away from him, and he could tell she was struggling to rein in her emotions. "He can't be trusted."

Calvin tried not to be distracted by Mia's outfit. When she left this morning, she had on jeans and a t-shirt. She came home in a black knee-length dress that gripped her curves as though she was born wearing it, and heels that made her long legs seem like they went on forever. "All I've done is agree to sit down with him and my parents one more time."

Mia closed the laptop she'd been sitting in front of for the last hour. "Don't let them keep using your brother's memory against you. Always following your first mind is what saved your ass and mine. Don't let your parent's desire for this to happen cloud your judgement."

Calvin frowned, almost missing her point because he was more into wondering why she was wearing one of her best—and sexiest—outfits to work. Normally, the shoes she kept in the armoire were for special events and date nights. Wasn't she watching someone's child? What would make her change *before* she made it home when she had enough time once she came through the door. "Like I said, out of respect for

Shawn and my parents, I took the meeting. But it was only to make it clear that I couldn't take on a consultant position."

Mia slipped her heels back on, and he watched every move. "I need you to use that Harvard brain and not your heart on this matter."

He cringed behind that statement.

"He's using your parents' grief to get next to you," she warned. "We agreed that you would continue working with Daron and the Castle, because we know what they stand for. Has something changed?"

"Sweetheart." Calvin inhaled deeply knowing that Mia had hit the heart of the matter. He still felt guilty that the Emperor's Suit wasn't being used by the people who he'd originally designed it for. The soldiers who had served alongside his brother were still risking their lives without something he'd created to improve the chances of survival for the hostages and all the rescuers.

Mia favored him with a steely glare. "I just lost someone that I thought I'd be trading future stories with. About our stubborn husbands and unruly kids and all that. I don't want you getting involved with someone like Gabriel. He'll quadruple the risk of me burying you next to your brother before we finally say I do."

Calvin tried to pull her close, but she side-stepped him and aimed for the bed.

"You put your life on the line every day for work," Calvin countered, checking his watch to see if it was time to go. "I'm the one who should be concerned."

She swiped a matching purse off the bed, then pushed him toward the door. "Ninety percent of my assignments are not half as dangerous as when people decide to make you and your inventions a target."

"I'm doing no such thing." He planted a quick kiss on her lips, trying to diffuse a little of her argument. "Look, this is the first time my parents have been back in Chicago since Shawn died. I don't think I was emotionally prepared for the impact it would have on me. I appreciate you keeping me grounded."

She walked down the hallway heading for the stairs. "We balance each other."

"You're looking gorgeous as always." Calvin's eyes devoured her body. "Why were you all dressed up when you came home?"

"We took Toya to a matinee play," Mia explained with a nonchalant shrug.

"Mmmmmm." That explained it, but Calvin only wanted Mia to dress like that when she was with him.

Mia's cut her eyes at him. "What's going on with you?"

He knew better than to share his true thoughts, so switching gears would be the best way to go. "Daron approached me about being a Knight and heading a project in Durabia."

Mia whipped around staring at him. "Durabia?"

The words were nearly a shriek, and before he had a chance to explain, she went in.

Mia placed her hands against his chest. "Durabia, though? Right now? We chose South Holland as a place to reside and raise a family because of their faith and family motto," Mia said as they made their way down the stairs. "We wanted to be tethered to an environment that fits what we desire to have in our future, despite all the security protocols we have in our house."

She was right, the place was drastically different from their fast-paced lives in the city. South Holland was a town with distinctive laws due to its roots as a Dutch Reformed Church settlement. Many businesses closed on Sundays, and the sale of alcohol was prohibited. As Mia had learned more about the history of her home, she told him that she found it interesting that when she searched for information on the Dutch Reformed immigrants in Wikipedia, Calvinism came up, which was another name for reformed Christianity. She said it was a sign that they'd picked the right location. In truth, she liked their motto of faith, family, and future in a time she was focused on reconnecting spiritually and laying the groundwork to start a family.

"It's not like we're planning to have kids right now." Calvin should have discussed the possible move to Durabia with her before this. It never occurred to him that Mia would have an issue with him taking on the project. But originally the scope was not supposed to take him out of the States. Being overseas could put a damper on their plans.

"Not right now but it was supposed to be in the near future." Mia ran those freshly manicured fingers through her hair, something she did when trying to contain her frustration. The heat rolling off Mia's glare had Calvin choosing his words carefully.

"I thought we'd enjoy being married a couple of years before adding to our family."

"That was the plan before we kept pushing back the wedding date," she countered, leaning on the entryway into the foyer. "I'm not trying to have children when I'm too old to enjoy them."

"Sarah had a child at ninety," Calvin joked, grabbing the car keys off the end table.

"Boy, I know you're not trying to use the Bible on me," Mia shot back, setting the alarm before they made it to the garage. "When was the last time you cracked open one, let alone stepped foot in a church."

"You act like you didn't just start going back." Calvin settled her on the passenger side before sliding behind the wheel to continue.

Mia gave him a hard glare. "Honey, don't try to veer away from the main issue. Nailing down a wedding date will be the least of our problems if you get involved with Gabriel London."

"Don't worry. I'm well aware that he's dangerous." Calvin couldn't lie, he was curious about what Gabriel had in store, if only to make sure he'd recognize the same project if he tried to get it through back door channels. But maybe she was right. This might be a risk that wasn't worth it. Maybe.

"I don't want to be planning a funeral instead of a wedding."

Well that sentiment went both ways.

Chapter 9

Calvin glanced at his phone as they sat in the car preparing to head into their event. His parents had called him three times today trying to arrange yet another meeting with Gabriel. The fact that the man who claimed to want his help wouldn't give him a general description of the project put him on edge. Calvin had no clue whether he was working on a protective device, a weapon, or a drone.

Sitting down with Gabriel was just to give his parents the appearance that he was trying. They were finally finding purpose in living and allowing themselves to enjoy life again. If meeting with a man he had no intentions of working with kept them on that path, then he'd do just that. Regardless of whether anyone else understood or not.

"Oh, I invited Avant out so that you could officially meet him," Mia threw out in a casual tone.

"Your *best friend* from high school?" He waited until she accessed the cameras outside the garage to make sure it was safe to exit. "He's in town?"

"He is." Mia's eyes widened as she hit the button to open the door. "He's part of the security assignment I'm on. I told you."

"No, you didn't mention that part," he said, filtering through the last conversations they had around the subject. "I know you *thought* you saw him the first night when we met up with my parents. You only talked about Toya and Emily. When did you see Avant?"

"Is it that you don't think I mentioned it or that you're so caught up in things that you weren't listening?" Mia asked in a tone he hadn't heard from her before. Accusatory with an underlying sentiment that something wasn't right.

"If you had said his name, trust me, I'd remember," Calvin fired back. True, their talks had been shorter than normal, because he'd been working more. He filtered through the conversations again looking for a moment where maybe he had been distracted and missed her saying Avant's name. No, he definitely would have remembered. "Maybe you intentionally didn't mention it."

"What are you trying to say?" Mia snapped.

"I said exactly what I meant to say."

Mia twisted in her seat so she faced him head on. "Hold up. What reason would I have not to tell?"

"That's exactly my question. Why do I know about Toya and Emily but you failed to mention Mr. Avant."

The short drive to the wine tasting hosted by a couple they met playing volleyball at the community center wasn't enough time for a full-on response. She left the car before he could open the door for her, taking long strides to make it to that red brick building. He could barely keep up.

"This thing with your parents really has you twisted," she said in a low tone but it was loud enough for him to hear.

"Oh dear, don't try to deflect." Calvin followed her into the dimly lit rustic restaurant, past the hostess stand into a private room. The entire back table was filled with a variety of wine and surrounded by people.

Mia gave him a stern look. "We're not about to do this right now."

"We have nothing but time to discuss why you chose not to tell me about your old flame." Calvin grabbed two samples of red wine and held one out to her.

Mia ignored it for a moment as her face lit up as a tall bearded man, a shade darker than ivory, wearing a navy shirt and white slacks crossed the room toward them. He had that kind of swagger that drew the attention of some of the women as he passed by. No, Mia did not mention this man at all.

"Hey, Avant. Glad you could make it out." Avant gave her a hug and kiss on the cheek, then smirked in Calvin's direction as he pulled her close—too close.

Calvin tensed, nearly ready to punch his smug face. The way Avant touched Mia was way too familiar and comfortable for them not to have seen each other for years. Even when they pulled apart, his arm was still around Mia's waist.

"This is my fiancé, Calvin." Mia playfully tapped Avant on the arm before finally taking one of the wine glasses from Calvin. "Calvin, this is my high school bestie, Avant."

"So, this is the nutty professor who stole your heart." Avant was still standing next to Mia making them look more like the couple and Calvin the third wheel.

"Nice to finally meet you." Calvin ignored the jab and shook the man's extended hand ignoring the unnecessary grip and attempt to intimidate.

"Do you remember when we got in trouble for drinking your mother's special wine?" Avant pulled out a chair at a nearby table and took a seat.

Mia made an attempt to sit, but Calvin gave her a look that halted that move. Instead, he pulled out her chair, then waited until she lowered into the cushion before claiming the space next to her. Avant's smirk disappeared as he had settled in.

"That was one time I was more scared of my mom than my dad." Mia laughed as a waiter placed three glasses in front of each of them on top of little cards with information on the type of wine they contained.

Avant rested his hand over Mia's. "Your mom was such a sweetheart."

Calvin gave it a few moments before extracting her hand from Avant's and placing it firmly within his own. Avant narrowed a gaze on him and Calvin favored him with a smile, then placed his arm around the back of her chair. He was grateful as a tall brunette wearing a mint green halter dress approached the table. "I'm glad you made it out."

She gave a rundown of how the event worked, but her eyes kept drifting to Avant as she spoke. That is, until she was called away by her boyfriend and co-host. The brief conversation with the hostess was enough to break up Avant and Mia's stroll down memory lane, but the "bestie" was aiming to get a rise out of Calvin by overstepping his boundaries.

"Are you in town for business or pleasure?" Calvin asked.

"Originally came for business but it has turned out to be … a bit of both." Avant sipped his wine then smiled at Mia over the glass. She averted her gaze and that move right there put Calvin on notice. He hadn't needed that warning from her father, but he was grateful all the same. Avant was gunning for his woman, and Mia was not immune to his charm.

Mia's male friendships had not bothered him until this moment. She worked in a male-dominated field. But this right here was something entirely different. While he didn't like it, Avant was only in town for a short period of time, right?

Mia picked up and read the card under the blush wine before taking a sip. "Was Toya knocked out when you left?"

Calvin tried not to react to the new information signaling that Avant was the guardian of the child she'd been watching over. Mia had some serious explaining to do. He definitely didn't like the look of longing in Avant's eyes.

And was that a flush of color in Mia's cheeks?

Chapter 10

Daron Kincaid had called Calvin right as they were leaving the restaurant last night. Mia slipped out of the house bright and early the next morning. They needed to finish the conversation about that move to Durabia, and she was certain he was aiming to grill her about Avant. That would have to wait, because Cameron had set up a meeting with Tyler at Cameron's cafe.

She followed Cameron through the front-end smoothie bar and into the smaller café. Once in the more intimate area, the wall gave her a good vantage point to both the smoothie bar and the gym lobby, even though the space couldn't be seen from the other side. In all the visits to Cameron's gym facility, she hadn't even noticed the bistro-style café.

"This will give you some privacy." Cameron guided Mia to a metal table. A few minutes later Tyler entered through a door Mia had barely noticed.

The young lady behind the counter greeted her, took her order, then led the way over to Mia.

Mia stood, taking in the woman's athletic form. "Thank you for coming."

Tyler lowered herself into the chair. "When someone reaches out with information that they really shouldn't have, I kind of feel obligated to come." She touched her ear, pulled out a phone, then glanced back at the door.

Mia watched as Cameron replaced the lady behind the counter who quickly disappeared into the back. Cameron grabbed the drinks and set them on the table before returning to stand behind the counter.

"Why are you following Avant?" Mia asked.

"First, who are you, really?" Tyler stuffed the cell into her pocket. "I know you work for Crossroads, but I didn't expect my communication line with my team to be jammed at this meeting."

"Considering the nature of what you were looking into, I just wanted to make sure this was indeed a private conversation." Mia had no idea Cameron had secured the room, but she wasn't shocked, either. At times, Cameron Stone was like the female version of Daron—resourceful and deadly.

Tyler scanned the café as if to confirm the level of privacy. "His cousin Leticia is connected to a person of interest in a deadly scheme."

"And you're thinking Avant may be a target." Mia sipped the turmeric, ginger, and chai mixed tea. Her mind flashed back to Calvin accusing her of intentionally not telling him about Avant. A tinge of guilt filtered through her mind, but she shook it off. Judging by the way Calvin and Avant squared off last night, that was probably the best idea.

"We're watching to see if anyone reaches out to him." Tyler glanced at Cameron who was making an attempt to appear severely interested in the cleanliness of the countertop.

Mia mulled over the information Cameron had given her before asking, "You're not sure of the recruitment process."

"We're not a hundred percent. We need to get someone in on the inside." Tyler stirred the tea but didn't partake. "The trail keeps leading back to innocent people. We've nicknamed them the murk group, because they are killing people's lives in one way or another."

"You have enough evidence to suggest something's amiss."

"But not enough to prove their innocence," Tyler added, finally taking a sip of the hot brew. "Avant doesn't fall into their profile for a main target. That's why we have eyes on him to see if we've missed something. But they still could want him to be part of the team."

Mia pulled out her phone to key in a few notes. "What's the profile?"

"Workaholic with little or no social life."

Hell, that sounded like Calvin before Mia met him. Well, lately still like him.

Tyler glanced toward the door as if she was expecting company. "Even though Avant doesn't have a social media presence, he has a full social life when he's not traveling on business."

"Is there anything specific you need to know? Maybe I can help get the information." Mia listened as Tyler gave her more details.

"FYI, Leticia is rumored to have accepted payment to send Toya with Avant. The robbery was staged to provide her a valid excuse."

"Isn't she in Texas?" Mia couldn't understand why anyone would need a ten-year-old to be with Avant when there were several other places the little girl could have gone. It didn't make sense.

"She is, but she's staying with the person rumored to have paid her." Tyler pulled out her wallet laying a few bucks on the table.

Mia glanced over in time to see Cameron tap her wrist. "I'll do some snooping."

She stood, looking through to the other side and found a man pacing in the smoothie bar area. "I probably should go before they do something drastic to get to me."

"Thanks for meeting," Mia said. "I'll get back to you as soon as possible."

Tyler pushed through the same door she'd entered earlier. Another man pulled a baseball cap low over his dark brown face. The slender man in the smoothie bar exited and joined both of them in the parking lot.

Cameron moved toward Mia. "Tread lightly. You don't want to draw attention to anything outside of Avant."

"Understood." Mia knew the two men showing up proved that Tyler and her boyfriend were working together. She wouldn't want to put Calvin on their radar. "Let me get to work. Thanks for setting this up."

Chapter 11

Thirty minutes later, Mia was walking up the stairs leading to the brick townhouse. Toya flung the door open and grabbed her hand, saying, "You're late."

Mia pushed the door closed behind them when the smell of apple, cinnamon, and fresh roasted coffee hit her. "Something smells delicious."

"Avant said your favorite breakfast treat used to be apple pancakes with apple syrup, so we made them."

"Did you now?" Mia allowed herself to be pulled into the kitchen by the exuberant bundle of energy. How could anyone resist such a beautiful little child. And Avant was out of touch—blueberry was her thing now.

"I'm so excited that we're going to Great America today," Toya said, climbing onto the stool and carrying on with her meal.

"Where's Emily?" Mia scanned the area and didn't see any of the nanny's personal items.

"It's just the three of us today." Avant smiled and a little bit of what he looked like as a teen came through.

"No, it's four. Rachel's going," Toya said, stuffing a piece of turkey sausage in her mouth.

"Yes." Avant leaned on the island next to Mia. Their bodies just inches apart as Toya finished her food and raced off toward the upstairs.

"Remember how we came to love this specialty?"

"Diana had gotten her aunt's ID taken at the club. We had to do a covert op to get it back." Mia couldn't forget. Her dad had revoked all privileges for an excruciating two weeks. But, at least Diana's aunt had her property returned.

"You two distracted the bouncer while I retrieved it." Avant slid the syrup toward her. "I deserved a good meal after that."

"We ended up there for hours running our mouths and eating apple pancakes." Mia drizzled syrup over the fluffy delicacies then took a bite. Good, but not as good as the ones Calvin made from time to time.

Avant stood, clearing the other plates. "We both got in trouble for that late-night escapade."

Mia forgot how delicious these were. She hadn't had them for years.

"This situation with Leticia has me paranoid. I could've sworn someone was following me yesterday." Avant returned to the island. "I felt foolish when the person went into the house next door."

She thought that over a moment, and given the circumstance being cautious was a good thing. "Nothing wrong with that but next time circle the block to make sure you're not being followed. If they continue to trail you, drive to the nearest police station."

"Hope I never need to do that."

Mia wiped her hands on a napkin. "I meant to ask, what is it that you do?"

"My title is financial consultant," he replied smoothly, grabbing the sunglasses off the counter and sliding them into the collar of his blue polo. "Mostly I'm a well-paid analyst and on occasion an accountant."

"So, how did you end up there?" Mia stared at his profile still amazed her friend had become so naturally sexy. "Diana mentioned that a nine-to-five wasn't your thing."

Toya bound back into the kitchen. "Is it time?"

"By the time you grab the snack bag, Mia should be done with breakfast and your cousin should be here." As if on cue, the doorbell rang. Avant glanced at his phone. "Are you ready for two rambunctious kids and stomach dropping rides?"

"Of course. I'm just your wingman. You'll have to do all the heavy lifting." Mia smiled as he rounded the counter and reached the front of the house. "And I'm not getting on any rides. I need the pancakes to stay put."

Mia had lied. She wasn't ready for the drive, which was filled with hundreds of questions including the repetitive ones of 'are we there yet'. The park was crowded for a Wednesday in July as they made their way toward the family rides. She asked him again about accounting since he hadn't answered the question.

"My route into accounting was a little backward." He grabbed hold of Toya as she veered off to look at the stuffed animals. "As I mentioned, I got off track in college. I would've changed majors, but I got a job as a financial analyst and it sparked my love of numbers. The accounting statement sheet didn't seem so boring."

"You always did have a love for numbers," Mia said as they moved forward into the line for the twirling teacups. Supposedly the "safe" rides that would keep them level to the ground. Not like those monstrosities that didn't seem to end without touching the sky first.

"It's paid me well." Avant leaned on the metal rail. "I plan to retire in a few years."

She watched people being spun around like little toy tops as the girls chattered with excitement. "Must pay very well for you to do that."

"Yeah, that and savvy financial planning." Avant glanced at her as the crowd shifted forward taking them along with it. "I'm working hard while I'm single. Hopefully when I settle down, I'll actually get to enjoy my family."

"You seem to have a lot of free time for a man in town on business," she hedged.

"There was a miscommunication," Avant responded as they finally made it near the front. "My boss declined a client, but his assistant put it on my schedule instead."

Mia followed the two girls who took off running to the nearest empty teacup. "Do you research your clients before working with them?"

"I assume my company does." Avant settled in next to Mia and pulled the bar down onto their laps. "They wouldn't take on anyone who would give them a bad rep."

Mia raised her arms as the attendant walked around tugging on the silver bars to make sure everyone was secured. "How long has this assistant been at the company?"

"About six months. Our normal person was injured in a car accident so we have a temp," Avant replied as the ride slowly took off.

"Do you have any special skill sets that your coworkers don't?" Mia smiled as the two girls screamed the minute the teacup picked up speed.

"Not really. I get assigned to certain accounts because of my ability to recall facts and figures without needing a computer, which helps when meetings take place in remote areas."

The ride slammed Mia into Avant's hard body. She attempted to hold onto the bar and stay on her side, but it was useless.

"Just stop trying." Avant's laughter filled her ear, as he slid an arm around her shoulder.

Mia felt like this was more of a family outing than work. Spending time with the girls and Avant had been amazing. The girls' playfulness, joy, and lightness were contagious. Reconnecting with Avant had brought her back to the point where it felt like they hadn't been apart for years. What she was experiencing with Avant and Toya and that sense of family was what she hoped to experience with Calvin. If she could keep him out of the labs and away from new assignments long enough. It also drilled in the fact that this was also what she would be losing out on if Calvin went to Durabia.

Would Calvin be satisfied and happy staying stateside and working on other projects? Or would the call of the newest project always be too hard to ignore?

* * *

"Uh oh." Avant touched her hand as he drove back. "That is not the reaction I was expecting to the fun day in the park."

"No," Mia glanced back at the two sleeping girls in the back seat. "I was thinking about work stuff."

"Let me get Rachel in the house." Avant pulled into driveway, then lifted the sleeping girl and carried her to the door.

Mia was grateful but sad that she had only a few more days to spend with them. Toya would leave town next week. One thing she knew for sure, it wasn't a good idea to maintain contact with Avant other than checking in on occasion. Calvin had almost punched Avant's lights out at dinner. That was after he laid on the threat that if Avant touched her one more time …

When he returned to the car, Mia asked, "How's Leticia?"

"I'm going to be honest with you." His eyes shifted to the rearview mirror. "Leticia's story about what happened keeps changing."

"What do you mean?"

"I believe something happened, but she's not being completely honest." Avant looked over in the direction of Toya. "I'm wondering if she just needed a break and she amped up the story to convince me to keep the little one for two weeks."

"What if she's not?" Mia asked, trying not to give any indication that she had information to collaborate his suspicions.

"Does it make sense that a robber would cross state lines to threaten a child to keep her mother from being a witness? Especially when they had a direct line of sight on the mother herself." Avant glanced over at her as he parked the car.

"Then why did you hire security?" Mia checked to make sure Toya was still sleeping.

"Initially, the officer I spoke to corroborated the threat, but when I recently tried following up on the case ..." Avant cut the engine, frowning. "I wasn't given that same feeling."

Mia peered at him. "So why am I still here?"

"Because Toya and I enjoy your company." Avant gave her a sly grin. "And there's no harm in having you present. You know, just in case I'm wrong."

Chapter 12

After spending the last few days researching and brainstorming, Calvin was moving forward with testing his concepts with a 3D print replica of Durabia.

"I hear you're barely using the team I acquired for you." Daron approached the center of the lab and thought his expression was neutral, but his tone was not.

Nicco Wolfe, who was guarding Calvin, nodded at Daron then stepped into the hallway to give them some privacy.

"I plan to. I've narrowed it down to two designs." Calvin handed Daron an octagon shaped piece of plastic that he developed for one of the shield concepts. "This and a liquid-to-solid design." He pulled out the notebook with several sketches he'd made over the last few days.

"I know you're used to working alone, but this is your moment to step up and be a leader." Daron looked over the replica, nodding. "Use your team, allow them to learn from you, to see the process and be an active part of the development of this shield."

Calvin grabbed his notebook and pen, jotting down some notes and questions. "I'll work on the first design and give them the second one. It requires more manpower to develop the prototype and test against the various agents."

"Do you always write everything on paper?" Daron studied the sketches of Calvin's shield, then glanced at his legal notepad, spiral notebook, and the portfolio.

"Yes, it helps me to bring things into focus. I'll input into the computer later and send it over to the team," Calvin answered. Brainstorming always worked best on paper first then creating a digital file later. He could go through several renditions before he finally committed to something that was close to the final.

"Stop by my office before you leave. I have a device that allows you to write in a book, and it records data onto a memory card for easy upload." Daron pulled out his cell, and keyed some information in. "Is everything solid with Mia?"

His head shot up from his notes and he glared at Daron. "Why would you even ask something like that?"

"Because this project will put a strain on your relationship. And it's not a good sign that you're here working late—again. And to be honest, it's not even necessary at this point." Daron returned the phone back to his jacket.

"I was so close to figuring out the liquid layer dynamics of my first plan. If I can get the concept nailed, I can better supervise the team development of the second one." Calvin felt bad about missing out on volleyball with Mia, but the more he worked out things on stateside the less time he'd have to spend overseas.

"You may want to pay a little more attention to Mia before you find yourself fighting to win back the woman you love," Daron warned. "Ask me how I know."

"We're good," Calvin said with confidence. She wouldn't be pleased with the Durabia project, but they hadn't really discussed the situation given the fact that she was out of the house at ungodly hours of the morning. Probably a good thing with the trouble his parents had stirred up and her comments on starting a family.

Daron stared at Calvin. "Don't ever get too cocky."

Roc, one of Daron's security personnel, knocked on the door. "Can I speak with you for a minute?"

"Sure." Daron stepped outside, leaning in the doorway.

Calvin stood, grabbing his back pack from the desk against the wall. Daron let loose with a profane word, and it snapped Calvin to attention. Daron was always calm under pressure. And rarely, if ever, cursed.

"The client that you asked me to follow up on has been working from home. Only going out briefly for meetings, then returning to the house." Roc whipped out his tablet and put his focus on the screen before turning it to face Daron. "Sometimes he appears to take the entire day off."

"While Mia's a grown woman, I didn't assign her to spend time with a single man." Daron glanced at Roc's device. "She should only be seeing him in passing. If he does it tomorrow, text me immediately."

Calvin snatched his phone from the table and checked the security feeds. Mia's car wasn't in the driveway or the garage. Then, with a twinge of guilt, he remembered she'd be at volleyball without him.

Daron reentered the room. "Sorry about that."

"Is everything all right?" Calvin rewound the house's security feed on his phone, but it didn't show Mia coming in. She could have gone straight there, but he had no way of knowing for sure. He was tempted to turn on her tracking earring to confirm her location, but doing so in a non-emergency situation would be invasive.

"I'm not sure yet. I need to dig into it and make sure there's not a problem." Daron pulled out his tablet from his inner jacket pocket. "But you do need to wrap up and go home, spend some time with Mia. This will be waiting for you tomorrow."

After what Calvin overheard, he wasn't going to argue. Especially since he knew something Daron did not.

Avant and Mia had history.

Chapter 13

Calvin hadn't been paying enough attention. Mia and Avant had only reconnected less than a week ago. Nothing between them had changed that would give him a reason to be concerned, but if Daron was feeling some kind of way… then Calvin should take that under consideration.

Mia entered the house. A basket of jasmine candles were lit and a spread of sugar scrub, body cream, bath bombs and face mask were waiting for her on the table. And the dining table with a spread of her Mediterranean favorites.

"What is this?" Mia smiled, dropping her bag on the couch.

"One of the things I missed was having dinner together, just the two of us." He noticed that she was still in her jeans and t-shirt from earlier as he pulled out a chair. She must not have gone to play volleyball. "How was your day?"

"It was good." Mia touched his forehead with her fingertips.

"What?" He frowned. "Can't I pamper my beautiful wife to be."

"Yes." Mia lowered her gaze at her obvious attempt to say that he was ill. Mia settled herself into the seat he held out for her. "It's a perfect opportunity to talk about that whole Durabia thing."

Calvin cringed. This conversation wasn't a part of his plan for a romantic evening. He sighed, took the seat across from hers and gave her a brief overview of the project as they both dug in.

Mia's fork stopped midway to her mouth. "Did you say chemical warfare?"

"I did." Calvin poured more wine into her glass. "But ..."

"You're not using *this* technology for soldiers." Mia slid out of her chair and crossed the room, flipping the switch to activate secure mode which didn't allow communication in and out of the room, something either one of them did when they were both in residence. She returned to the table.

"No, but it's where I started."

Mia had been so patient, understanding and accommodating with his work ethic when it came to projects. Calvin didn't want her to think marriage wasn't a priority. But accepting this project required him—or them to set foot in Durabia to make his concepts a reality. No getting around it.

She positioned both hands over her mouth as though sending up a prayer. "This is what you've been working on."

"My idea was to make a device that protects individual soldiers during a chemical attack, but now I've been assigned to produce a larger scale to protect an entire city," Calvin said, then explained the protective shield concept along with the reason Durabia needed one. An American woman who was the beloved of Kamran Ali Khan, a former crown prince, had been kidnapped by the Sheikh of Nadaum. She freed herself by using her wits and courage but left the Sheikh in such a state that the entire Muslim world was up in arms. Now there is a bounty on her head with a target on the peaceful country of Durabia. Bringing Khalil, the Kings and the Knights in was how Kamran was doing everything in his power to keep everyone safe.

"I can see in your eyes that you really want to do this, but this will be more dangerous than what happened with your earlier inventions," Mia said, and the anxiety in her eyes was clear.

Calvin took her hands in his. "This project would have a huge effect on both of our lives. It's an awesome privilege to create something of this magnitude. And unlike America, who also has their hands in the dirt, and some other Middle Eastern countries, who already are using questionable protection measures, Durabia is attached to The Castle. That means they've been vetted by Khalil and the Kings. If they're asking me to do this, Durabia really needs it and will use it only as intended."

"So how long will you be there?" Mia folded her arms across her chest.

Calvin immediately took note she didn't say *we* and his heart sank. "They're thinking anywhere from one to three years. But I'd only need to be there for six months to make sure the configuration works. Then I'd probably go for one week a month for testing until we work out all the kinks."

After that, Calvin was sure Daron's team could take care of the rest, and he could handle most issues remotely.

Mia released a long, slow breath. "We finally get our schedules to a point where we're spending time together. And now you want to take on an assignment that puts miles between us." Mia lifted the wine glass, taking a huge sip.

"You could come with me."

"I finally feel like I have a life outside of work," she shot back. "Now you want me to move to a place where the culture is not kind to women like me." Mia poured herself another glass of wine, nearly filling it to the brim before the bottle slammed against the wooden table. "It's one thing to do an assignment or two there, even visit for a short period. But to move there while you work hour after hour in a place that is not governed the same way as the States, leaving the life we are building behind, is not ideal."

"Maybe you could go back to being on my security team for the duration of the project," Calvin suggested. "You'll be under a different set of rules."

"Protecting you on U.S. soil while you work on this will be a challenge, trying to protect you on foreign soil makes me extremely uneasy." Mia closed her eyes and took a couple of breaths. "But you're already working on it, so we're already in danger."

"No one knows that I'm working on it except Daron, Kamran Khan, Khalil Germaine, and the rest of the Kings, and we know they won't say anything."

Mia twisted her engagement ring as if she was ready to rip it off. "Clearly we're not on the same page about starting a life and being a family. So, I'm going to go back to being a single woman."

"What are you talking about?" Calvin's heart drop to the pit of his stomach.

"From what I researched about the Middle East, unmarried couples are not allowed to live together or share a room. And since we won't be tourists in a hotel, how is that supposed to work out for us?" She stood, walked away from the table and headed upstairs.

Calvin blew out the candles and followed her. If he gave her space now, he might find her walking out of his life permanently.

"I don't want us to do a long distance relationship." Calvin almost wished she'd yell at him, this layer of anger under the calm scared him. "We could get married before we go."

Mia spun around. "I don't want to rush to the altar because you accepted an assignment in a foreign country. In a city that I can't kiss you or hold your hand in public because I could get arrested."

"We will—"

Mia put her palm up. "I'm not going to Durabia to end up being alone. You working long hours while I'm doing what? What happens to my life while you're off trying to protect a place where you don't even live?"

"Maybe it's convenient for you to be single at this point in time." Calvin moved closer to her.

Mia pinned him with a *what the hell* look, and crossed her arms. "Are we waiting three years to start a family? Because I didn't think that was the plan. Or is this your way of saying, despite what you promised, work is going to take the front burner again?"

"That's not what I was trying to say." Calvin pulled her to him. "Honestly, I messed up. I didn't fully factor in the implications to our lives in my decision. I was focused on the pros and cons of the project itself."

"Well, now you have to deal with the fallout." She slipped away, went into the guest room and slammed the door.

Chapter 14

The next morning, Mia paced in front of the island, frustrated that
Calvin would make such a huge decision without discussing it with her
first. As if her life would not be greatly impacted. When he said Durabia,
she thought they might need him for a couple of weeks, months, maybe,
but not years. He was being too damn optimistic to believe that he could
do six months then hand it off for someone else to build. He was too
possessive of his inventions. Which meant he'd likely be in Durabia for
the full duration. Precious time they didn't have.

"Let me run up and see if Toya is still on with her mom." Emily's
voice snapped her out of her reflections.

"I'll head up." Mia slid her tablet into her tote and trotted up the
wooden stairs. She paused near Toya's cracked bedroom door.

"Did you ask your cousin to take you?" Letica asked via video chat.

Toya shifted the iPad on the desk. "Yes, but he hasn't answered yet."

"Baby, you only have a few days left before you come home." Leticia
glanced behind her then focused back on Toya. "It's very important you
get him to take you."

Toya twisted in the chair. "Mom, it's okay. I don't have to go."

Mia tried her best to see who was in the corner of the screen behind
Leticia but she didn't want them to know she was listening.

"I need you to do this for me." Leticia turned and whispered something to someone offscreen. "I'll have a special treat for you when you get back."

"Okay, I will."

"That's great baby," Leticia said, beaming. "Just call me when he says yes. Then tell me what time he's taking you. Now what did you do this morning?"

Mia kept moving down the hall to Avant's room to find out where Toya had been trying to get him to take her. She didn't understand why anyone would place a child with him as a method to get close. She had scanned Toya's items for tracking and listening devices and found none. However, getting Avant in a location that would put him at ease and not arouse suspicion was the only viable option she came up with. She knocked on the door but didn't get a response.

"Avant, I need to speak to you for a moment." She waited a few moments and nothing happened. *He's probably still getting ready for his meeting.*

Avant cracked open the door with a towel draped around his midriff. Not what Mia was expecting. Her eyes dropped to his v-cut abs and muscular chest which still glistened with water. *Damn, this man shouldn't be so fine.* She immediately pivoted and tipped back in the opposite direction.

"Hey, did you need something?" Avant leaned against the door frame giving a sensual smirk. His grayish-blue eyes twinkled with mischief.

Mia averted her gaze as he slid a thumb beneath the knot in the towel. "Nothing that can't wait until you're fully dressed."

"You never wondered what we'd be like together," Avant whispered as he stepped closer, his eyes so filled with desire that she almost stopped breathing.

"Maybe a time or two after breaking up with boyfriends over the years, but I'm engaged now." Mia's thumb touched the platinum band as if she needed a physical reminder of the man who truly loved her.

"But you're not married yet." He tilted toward her. "Tell me you don't feel anything for me."

Mia felt a connection, an undeniable pull to the man who used to be one of her best friends. Of course, she felt something, but she was uncertain of what it was. "I'm not having this conversation with you half-naked with Toya two doors down." She spun him around and pushed him into the room then sped back down the hall.

As she passed Toya's room, a male voice caused her hasty steps to halt.

"Where did she say he was going?"

"A mix in a bee garden but he said he'll be home in time for us to watch The Princess and The Frog before I go to bed," Toya eagerly supplied.

"What the hell is that?" the man asked.

Mia couldn't hear Leticia's answer to the man, but she understood it was a business mixer at the botanical gardens.

"That's good baby," Leticia said. "But don't forget to ask him about Navy Pier."

Mia headed downstairs, firing off a text to Tyler about tonight and Navy pier. Emily had just taken their late lunch out of the oven when Mia made it to the living room.

"Is Toya still on with her mom?" Emily placed the pizza on the counter.

"She's wrapping up now." Mia's mind was flipping between the conversation she overheard and seeing Avant in that towel. Both were disturbing for different reasons.

Emily set the plates and a pitcher of sweet tea on the table. "Let me run up and get her. She'll end the call and start playing video games." She headed to the stairs, stopping as Avant hit the bottom one wearing a tailored blue suit that touched him in all the right places.

"Remember, I'll be in a meeting between four to six so call me back to back if it's an emergency." Avant checked his pockets and pulled out his cell. "I should be home around seven or eight."

"Okay." Emily smiled up at him as though suddenly in a trance. "Your tie is crooked," she said in a husky voice. "Let me fix it." She adjusted his perfectly straight tie then ran her hand over his bicep.

"Thanks." Avant stepped aside allowing Emily enough space to pass. She glanced back several times before making the journey upstairs. "Mia, I'll see you on Monday."

"We'll talk later." Mia would have to deal with this 'more than friends' conversation.

"I already received a call from your boss."

Mia frowned as the door slammed shut. She retrieved her device and pulled up the work file to see what the hell Daron had said to him. If Calvin had anything to do with this, the conversation would not be as calm as the Durabia one.

No notes in the file. She dialed Daron.

"Is there a problem?" Daron asked upon answering.

"That's what I'm trying to find out." Mia moved into the foyer as she heard footsteps heading her way. "You called the client today."

"It was brought to my attention that he hasn't been going in to work."

"*Who* brought it to your attention," Mia huffed. "Because it's been in the file from day one?"

Silence on the other end was not a good sign. "Now, I'm going to ignore your tone and simply ask, does it matter who I assigned to follow up?" Daron asked in a stern voice.

She silently cursed, reminding herself he was her boss, as well as a friend. She took a deep breath and tried to rein in her attitude. "I was trying to confirm that nothing had happened that I should be concerned about. He mentioned it, but left out for a meeting before we could discuss it."

"We'll see. Your assignment may change, but I'll let you know first thing on Monday." He followed with a "bye" then ended the call.

She squeezed the phone in her hand.

"Mia are you not going to eat with us?" Toya yelled from the kitchen.

Mia inhaled and exhaled before heading their way. "I'm coming."

"Emily said we're going biking on the Lakefront after this." Toya stuffed a few fries in her mouth.

"Yep."

"I wish Rachel could go." Toya's smile fell momentarily. "She's coming back before I go. Maybe Avant will take us to the Sky Zone."

"So, what do you want to do before you head home?" Mia felt guilty for secretly interrogating a ten-year-old, but Leticia could be putting Avant and Toya in danger with this Navy Pier business.

* * *

Four hours later, Emily, Toya, and Mia were laid out in the living room recovering from their lakefront adventure. Mia updated and closed out her report for the day. They were all surprised when Avant entered thirty minutes later.

"I expected you to be long gone." He dropped his keys in the glass bowl sitting on a table in the foyer.

"We stayed on the lakefront longer than planned," Mia said, glancing at her watch.

Toya was sleeping in the chair. Avant picked Toya up. "I'm going to take her to her room."

Emily gathered her things, then slid between Avant and the chair instead of going around like a normal person would. "I'm going to head out."

Mia walked to the door with her as Avant carried Toya upstairs. She watched as Emily made it to the rental car. A few minutes later, Avant returned and went straight into the kitchen.

"I thought you'd left," he said when he noticed her closing the distance between them.

"We need to talk."

"I apologize for earlier." He unbuttoned his jacket and loosened his tie. "I was out of line."

"Look, I'd like you to be a part of my life," she said. "But you have to respect that I have a man."

Mia wasn't ready to say goodbye to a friend who made her laugh and lightened her soul. A friend who understood things that she had to explain to others. Someone who helped her a great deal when she'd lost her mother while others were only offering sympathies. Mia hadn't cared, because Avant and Diana were there for her in every way she needed them to be.

"I can handle that." He pulled down a bottle of Moscato and poured two glasses. "I was the fool that didn't shoot my shot when I had the chance."

"Well, at least my guy isn't going to threaten to cut you if you don't stay away from me. At least I don't *think* he will." She laughed, making reference to one of his girlfriends from high school.

"I should've known you'd bring her up." He chuckled, sliding a glass her way. "She was cute and crazy as hell."

"Hell, the way Emily keeps sliding up on you. You'll need a bodyguard."

"That's why I got her a separate place instead of letting her stay in the third bedroom." He took a sip of wine. "I didn't want any problems."

Mia loved how they eased back into the rhythm of their friendship. She hadn't realized how much time had passed with them drinking and talking until her phone rang. Calvin. Shoot! She should have been home.

She answered and said, "I'm on my way."

Chapter 15

Calvin didn't like that Mia had lost track of time. That was not like her. He was counting down until she was off this assignment. Hopefully Daron had nipped Avant working from home in the bud, even if it meant placing her somewhere new on Monday.

"Hey beautiful, I ran you some bathwater." He kissed Mia on the cheek. "Walking all over the park probably has you tired."

Mia slipped out of her clothes. "Is this about yesterday?"

"With my parents and everything going on this week we've been out of sync. I wanted to pamper you a little," Calvin admitted, grabbing her a robe and leading her to the bathroom. "I picked up some of your favorite food from Uncle Julio's."

Mexican food? Bathwater? She smiled, peering in the bathroom. "Look at you with the scented candles lit and mood music."

"The water is going to be cold if you don't get in soon." Calvin's eyes scanned her body standing in only her skin-toned underwear.

"Is that right?" She leaned seductively in the doorway of the bathroom.

"If you don't take your sexy ass in here, we won't be eating until much later." He leaned toward her, lifting his eyebrows suggestively.

Mia gave a him a sly grin then grabbed the robe from his hand and closed the door.

He chuckled then went downstairs to put the food in the oven and set the timer on the phone. In the bedroom, he pulled out his laptop. He had been researching weather patterns, buildings, and landscapes that would factor into his new invention, but also wanted to look into Durabia's laws and activities. The goal was to figure out how to address Mia's concerns. The truth was they would most likely be living in the old Durabia, which had more restrictions than the more lenient Free Zone of new Durabia.

A notification pinged at the bottom of his computer. He clicked to open the message, and a video feed of his parents opened on the screen. Janine was passing out bags to a line of people. Bruce was setting a box down at the table. The scene was innocent enough, but his heart dropped as he slowly realized the implication of why it had been sent to him. His cell rang with an unknown number. He had one guess on the caller's identity.

"They're so sweet, it would really be a shame if a tragedy hit this event," Gabriel taunted.

Calvin's screen switched to another room where several people had formed an assembly line and were efficiently putting care packages together. White smoke leaked into the area as people coughed and ran for the door. Now he wished he hadn't changed his mind and had actually met with Gabriel.

"What exactly do you want?" Calvin's screen switched back to his parents who were smiling and laughing, unaware they were in danger. Only safe for the moment while Gabriel waited to see if he complied.

"I'll send you the details of where we meet tomorrow," Gabriel growled. "Don't bring an entourage."

Calvin stared at his parents wishing there was a way to discreetly warn them, or even make a call to Daron to bring the Kings in on this.

"I mean no one. And that includes your fiancée."

The bathroom door opened; Mia entered. "Are you all right?"

"Umm. Yes and no." Calvin quickly closed the laptop. "I need to process some things then I'll let you know where I land."

He didn't want to lie to Mia, but he also couldn't tell her. She would, without a doubt, get her entire team involved. He didn't want someone else coming in making the final call on whether he'd have to sacrifice his parents' lives for the greater good. Moving forward meant knowing if the product was a weapon or just a technology advancement.

Calvin had a plan. Unfortunately, he had to get through dinner without giving any of the new developments away.

Chapter 16

Calvin slid out of bed, glancing back to make sure Mia was still asleep. His mind was still racing. He couldn't concentrate on Durabia or Mia until he figured out how to get his parents safely back to Florida. He'd hired protection once they returned to the Chicagoland area, but it was too late to have someone watch over them in Wisconsin without getting them killed.

Hopefully, Mia would just think he was working. He slipped on a jogging suit and grabbed the laptop before heading down to his home lab. He threw some items that he thought he might need into a bag. Breaking into Gabriel's facility to look at the item in question was a dangerous venture, but it was essential to figuring out how to best help his parents.

He drove to the Hyde Park area where he switched to a Nissan Maxima that wasn't registered to him, then drove the rest of the way to the facility. Calvin had never been so grateful for Mia's decision to leave several cars stashed throughout the city for taking meetings with new clients. Calvin definitely didn't want to be in a vehicle easily traceable back to where he lived. He parked two blocks out then turned on the Emperor's Suit, slid the glasses on, then slipped covers over his shoes so the treads wouldn't leave imprints on any surface.

The glasses were normally used to see others who were wearing The Suit, but the glasses also had the ability to record. He adjusted his gloves as he watched the two guards take turns circling the building. Neither man had entered. Calvin stepped into the alcove near the door to be ready when someone opened. Fifteen minutes passed before one guard keyed in the code and Calvin followed him in.

The moment Calvin hit the hallway he knew he could have a problem passing the security room. One of the screens had heat signatures. He looked across at the lab, and the number of bodies in the room matched the heat signatures on the screen. Once he entered the lab, despite wearing a suit that made him invisible to the naked eye, he'd be seen. Gabriel clearly didn't want him making an unannounced visit. He made a mental note to make some alterations to the Emperor's Suit. Calvin searched the hallway until he found a first aid kit mounted on the wall, then he searched for a blind spot in the camera. He knocked the kit off the wall so the contents would spill on the floor, before kicking and sliding the items he needed into the camera's blind spot.

"What the hell? Is this place haunted?" One of the guards picked up the kit.

"Sometimes when they run those machines the wall shakes," the other guard said. "It probably was just loose and finally fell."

Calvin held the items from the first aid kit close to his body so that it was within the field of protection of his device. Once they left the hall, he made quick work of the ice pack and the cooling blanket and a few items he'd brought with him. This would keep his body temp from reading but he'd have to be smart about his movements. He wouldn't create a heat signature, but his cooler temp wouldn't exactly blend. He needed to make sure that it would look like an anomaly on the screen and not a cold body in the room.

He returned to the lab the moment someone left out. Immediately he crouched below the glass, scanning the area until he found what he was looking for. He stayed as low to the ground as possible as he made his way to the brunette at the computer.

Calvin scanned the different images of blankets on her screen.

Gabriel couldn't possibly be threatening his parents over a blanket. Using his glasses, he captured the images. His gaze shifted to scraps of material and foam in a glass case further down. Then his eye was caught by another glass box containing a flash drive and pictures. As he inched closer, he realized these items were essential to the project. Or at least that's what was suggested by the pressure plate that the items were set on. He hopped back as a man came over to the box.

"Do you think London will be able to get him to give up the secret to his protection pod?' He glanced back at the woman.

The brunette turned her chair. "Do you know how many teams he had working on this damn thing with no success?"

"Well, evidently they found someone to finish because people are willing to pay top dollar to have this." The guy stared at the case. "Where is it?"

"Where is what?"

"The prototype?" He keyed numbers in at the base of the case then lifted the lid.

She came over to where he stood. "Gabriel was the last one who had it in his possession. He had a meeting with one of the investors and they wanted to see the product and pictures."

"The pictures are here. The prototype is not." He pulled out his phone. "I need to take another look at the spine in the blanket."

One of the pictures slid to the floor and Calvin recognized an item he'd long forgotten about. A portable protection tent packed in a small square. The inspiration had been a pocket-sized blanket that he'd once taken to camp years ago. Calvin created the protection pod to be compact, but quickly expand to a tent. It could fit two to three people, depending on their size. The material was bullet proof with one transparent section to observe any outside activity. He figured it would give his brother just cause if he ever came under fire and couldn't find shelter. The pod had an interior zipper where Shawn could place a weapon in position to fire back if necessary.

"I still can't believe that same square turned into something that saved three people's lives." She scooped the picture from the floor.

"Yeah, but something tells me some of the details of that story have been altered just like that file on that flash drive." He shifted the items around in the box.

"Hey, my brother is a soldier." She pursed her pink lips and nearly glared at him. "I'd love for him to have one with him. That's why I am here."

The man swiped a finger to unlock his phone. "But he could do the same thing Shawn did, and use it to save someone else's life."

"I'm here because I wanted him to have that choice." She stalked away, reclaiming her place at the computer as he put the phone up to his ear.

Calvin made his way to the door. He had all the information he needed.

As he was about to exit, Daron and Mia entered the hallway, each had on an Emperor's Suit. He was glad he had on the glasses that allowed him to see them. Their focus was so intent on him that they probably didn't notice the heat sensor. Calvin rushed out of the lab to meet them before they hit the trouble zone. Mia looked like she was ready to snatch him seven ways to Sunday. Daron's expression reminded him of that time he snuck back in the house at nine in the morning and his father was waiting.

Neither of them said a word until they were away from the facility.

"How did you know I was here?" Calvin asked.

"I may not be a part of your protection team, but I make it my business to know your schedule," Mia fired back.

"Imagine my surprise when I get a call asking if there was a change in plans." Daron stopped walking to retrieve a drone.

Calvin glanced over at Mia's face which was taut with anger. "I just needed to do some research to figure out how to help my parents."

"By breaking into a lab." Daron shook his head.

"Wait, why am I just hearing that your parents are in trouble," Mia snarled.

Calvin knew he'd messed up. "I needed to figure out how—"

"See, that's the problem. *We* should've figured it out." She threw up her hands.

"I agree with Mia. You should've brought *us—*" He pointed between him and Mia. "—in on the initial planning. This is what we do."

"You could've gotten yourself killed or kidnapped, and I wouldn't have even known where you were." Mia turned to Daron. "Would you please make sure he gets home safely? I need to go clear my head."

"I'm not a child in need of babysitting," Calvin snapped. "Mia, I—"

He was talking to himself. She had slipped into a black sedan and drove off as Nicco pulled up in an SUV.

"What's going on with you man?" Daron motioned for Nicco to keep driving. "As a Knight, your actions directly affect The Castle."

"But you all—"

"Yes, we do stuff like this all the time. But we do it as a team. Like family. We. Do. Not. Go. Rogue."

Calvin hadn't realized until that moment how the betrayals in his life were still affecting him. "Honestly, I planned to tell you later."

"Where's your vehicle?" Daron glanced around. "We need to get out of here."

Gabriel London's car zoomed past, which suggested he wasn't aware the prototype was missing. That was not a good thing. The minute he found out, it would make the situation with his parents even more volatile.

Chapter 17

Calvin couldn't believe no one had informed his family that the protection pod he'd given his brother had been used to help save three of the hostages. Based on what Daron found out, Gabriel had been trying to duplicate Calvin's invention ever since. He had several entities offering him big money. The most ridiculous one was a million dollars for a single pod.

"You're right." Daron placed a projector on the coffee table, then pulled up the image of the building where the older Atwoods were staying. Cameron slid into the kitchen. "He'll probably have regular security and thermal imaging in play, which presents a problem."

"Maybe we can get your parents to leave the building to meet us," Mia suggested, dropping her duffle near the door before taking the spot on the couch next to Calvin—a few noticeable inches between them. Oh yes, she was still pissed. "They aren't aware they're in danger."

Calvin looked at the building schematics. "Gabriel isn't going to want them to leave. He may escalate things to keep them on the property."

Daron stopped typing on his tablet. "We definitely don't want him to get physical. That's why I suggest you set up the meeting with Gabriel at the Geneva Cove Hotel."

"He won't release the chemical while on-site," Mia said, patting Calvin's hand. "It'll give us a chance to get them safe."

"That's not true," Cameron said, leaning on the kitchen island sipping a cup of coffee out of Mia's favorite mug. "Gabriel isn't going to meet you in the same area as your parents. There is a chance he will release whatever this chemical agent is into the area your parents are in."

Daron shot her a 'what the hell' glare. "Cam."

"I don't believe in sugar-coating situations." Cameron met his glare head on. "That's how people end up six feet under. I'm trying to make sure we don't go in without considering all factors."

"So how are we doing this?" Calvin's phone pinged and he struggled to push aside Cameron's ominous words. He glanced down to see the details of the meeting coming through. "He wants to meet in Crystal Lake."

Daron took the phone reviewing the information for himself. "You need to change the location."

"Are we bringing law enforcement in?" Calvin asked.

"Not this time," Daron answered. "We need more time to figure out who his buyer is."

Cameron made her way to the sitting area and the four of them worked out a strategy that Calvin was confident was the best decision.

* * *

Several hours later, Calvin was sitting in a parking lot in Lake Geneva, fifteen minutes away from his parents' location. Daron and his team were already on-site. He tried not to rub the eye with the special contact lens and was already missing the glasses, because contacts didn't have recording capabilities.

"Are you in position?" Daron asked via the communication piece in his ear.

"Yes," he answered.

"You should be able to pull up the feed with the Kings."

He grabbed the tablet out of the glove compartment. On the screen, he could see the other eight Kings checking the vents in the area. They had been hoping that the access ports to the vents weren't in the main area, but that wasn't the case.

Shaz came on the line. "We're not going to be able to remove the chemical without them noticing."

They couldn't risk Gabriel's men attacking as they extracted the disbursement device.

"I'll have Nicco bring you the supplies to block the vents," Daron answered. "It looks like you're taking the meeting, Calvin."

Calvin slid the tablet back in the glove compartment before driving out of the lot, hating that they were moving to Plan B. The risk to his parents was much higher.

The stone building was beautiful, but the number of armed men stationed right outside the doors made him anxious. While it was a military event, no one seemed to think it was odd, even though it was an outreach fundraiser.

He took a deep breath, left the car, and moved toward Gabriel, who was surrounded by three armed men. They immediately pulled him inside the glass door and checked him for weapons. "Mr. Atwood, glad you could make the time."

"As if you gave me a choice."

Calvin followed him through the crowd of volunteers and into a corridor with fewer people.

Gabriel opened a metal door to an area with a single table with a laptop and two chairs. He pointed to the steel chair facing the computer screen which had a live stream of his parents working the event. "I hated going to such measures, but I have a deadline to meet. Trust me, I tried to do this without you."

"I'm supposed to pull a rabbit out my hat and fix your mystery product." Calvin was a little nervous about being in such a closed-off space. Gabriel's men easily could shoot him before any of Daron's men could make it through the door.

"I have every confidence that you can do it." Gabriel sat across from him and placed a black remote on the edge of the table in front of him. "Now here's what will happen. We've set up a room for you to work."

He tapped the laptop. "I just wanted to remind you what's at stake."

Calvin's eyes were glued to the screen. "So how much money do you stand to make off this?"

"I'm in your parents' room," Mia announced in his earpiece. "It looks like they were planning to leave early."

Mia hadn't wanted to be the one to pack up his parents' things, but she knew they wouldn't appreciate strangers doing it. It allowed her to escort them directly out of the room to their car.

"That is none of your concern." Gabriel lifted the remote. "If I press this, dear Janine and Bruce will be among the hundreds of people injured in a terrible attack. That is what you need to be worried about. Not my money."

Calvin relaxed as Cameron approached Janine on the screen. "That's debatable."

He refrained from sharing that he knew anything about the protection pod. Daron thought it would increase the risks. They didn't want to shoot their way out with his parents and so many innocent people on the property.

Gabriel's cell vibrated. "Is it ready?" He asked the person on the other end, then paused for a moment before his gaze shifted to Calvin. "We're on our way."

"Don't go," Daron ordered. "We just need a few more minutes to get your parents safely to the car and on the move."

"Where's the confidential agreement you mentioned?" Calvin asked, not knowing how to buy time.

"Is that really necessary?" Gabriel stood with the remote in his hand. "How about I lock the room your parents are in and release that gas?"

Calvin slowly made it to his feet. "Lead the way."

"Everybody's on the move," Daron declared and only then did Calvin feel an ounce of relief. "Cameron's coming to get you."

Ouch. That might not be the best thing. Cameron was known for shooting first and leaving no one alive to ask questions later.

One of the men held the door open for Gabriel. They filed out of the room, turning down the hallway. Calvin glanced back at the two armed men behind him. While he was wearing a bulletproof suit, he didn't think it was designed for assault rifles at close distance.

Cameron bumped Gabriel and the guard as she made her way down the hall.

"Watch where you're going," Gabriel growled, frowning over his shoulder at her.

"Gentlemen." Cameron did a one-eighty, leaned in and grabbed Calvin's wrist pulling him to her. "I'm going to have to steal this fella away from you."

Gabriel reached into his pocket as Calvin situated the gun that Cameron slapped in his hands. "It's a shame your parents have to die."

Chapter 18

"Are you looking for this?" Cameron held the remote control.

Gabriel went for his gun. "It seems you want to die in their place."

"I'm fine with not doing things nice and easy." Cameron whipped out two weapons, as the man next to Gabriel suddenly dropped and hit the floor, compliments of her quick shot.

The other men with Gabriel went for their weapons. "I wouldn't move unless you're ready to die."

"I suggest you find another way to finish your project," Calvin said.

Cameron angled the gun directly for the center of Gabriel's forehead. "Or I could put a bullet in him and make sure he never goes after your parents again."

Gabriel's hands inched up slowly.

"Don't make me regret not taking her up on that offer." Calvin slipped out of the door several inches away. Cameron followed after firing three shots.

"He's out, see you back at the house," Cameron said as she moved near Calvin.

Calvin froze, tried not to look at the men spread out on the ground. "I thought you weren't going to kill them."

"I didn't. They'll wake up in an hour or so." Cameron pushed him forward as they rushed toward his vehicle. "I'm not trying to get shot in the back."

"I'm with you on that." Calvin slid behind the wheel.

"We'll need to find a way to shut him down." Cameron continued to glance behind them. "Once you're on a plane to Durabia, it will keep you out of his line of fire. Then Daron would only need to protect your parents."

The door they exited was flung open. Several armed men came running out. He pressed the accelerator, creating more distance between them and the stone building. "You think he'll go after them again?"

Calvin wanted this situation to be over. Cameron may have had a point, but the idea of being overseas if Gabriel went after his parents again disturbed him. He also didn't like leaving Mia behind and giving Gabriel a chance to use her against him. At the end of the day, Calvin wondered if he should give Gabriel what he wanted simply for his own peace of mind. It wasn't like the protection pod was a weapon. All it would do was line Gabriel's pockets and protect some rich paranoid person. What was the harm in that?

"Depends on who is trying to purchase the protection pod." Cameron snatched the cap off her head, letting the auburn curls cascade down her back. "I'll get the details from Daron and look into it."

He took advantage of the drive home to get a little insight from Cameron. "How can I convince Mia to go to Durabia?"

"What reasons did she give for not consenting prior to you agreeing to the project?"

Calvin could name a few, but which one to say first?

She chuckled. "By your silence, that means you already made major miscalculations. That is not going to bode well for a favorable decision."

The conversation that followed Cameron's assertions was eye-opening. By the time Calvin was pulling into his garage, twenty minutes after Mia notified him that she had arrived at the house safely, he realized that he might have to go to Durabia alone.

When he entered his South Holland home, Mia and his parents were in the living room, and Daron was in the kitchen fixing pasta, salad, and garlic bread.

His mother hopped up from the couch and wrapped her arms around him. "I'm so sorry."

Cameron slid past him into the kitchen, and peered over Daron's shoulder into the pot.

"We realized you were telling the truth about him when this fell out of Gabriel's pocket." Bruce stood, handing over the protection pod he'd given his brother. Calvin hadn't laid eyes on it in years.

Janine's eyes brimmed with tears. "It led us to believe that he was in it for the money and not to save lives and honor Shawn's memory."

"Evidently Shawn used it to save three of the hostages," Calvin said, grateful that his parents were safe and still alive to drive him crazy. Now he had to wonder about the fact that the tent was still intact. Did he have something to do with his brother's death?

Bruce wrapped an arm around his wife's shoulder.

"Why didn't anyone tell us this?" His mother asked, wiping her face with the back of a trembling hand.

Mia came over to where they were standing. "I don't know, but for your safety don't speak to another soul about this or ask any questions."

Janine frowned. "But—"

"Mia's right." Calvin led them toward the couch. "We don't know who Gabriel is involved with. Shawn would not want you putting yourself in danger because of him."

"You and those King people will take him down." Bruce looked back toward the dining room where Daron and Cameron were setting the table. "Won't you?'

"I will not allow Gabriel London to profit off Shawn's death." Calvin would check in with Daron to see if there was anything he could do to aid the investigation. He certainly wanted Gabriel behind bars before he actually hurt someone in an attempt to acquire those millions.

The question remained. Who the hell was he working for?

Chapter 19

Mia's request to remain on assignment when Avant wasn't working was granted. Mostly because she told Daron about the call she overheard. Mia could see why they wanted Avant at Navy Pier. Tyler blended well into the crowd. If Mia wasn't a trained professional, she probably wouldn't have noticed the woman at the water park.

People milled around the pier as the blue waves of Lake Michigan smashed against the shore. Avant and Emily were watching Toya explore the Children's Museum, and Avant made small talk with several parents while checking out the permanent exhibits. Emily, who couldn't seem to keep her hands off Avant, or stop brushing her body against him, finally headed toward the restrooms.

Mia kept a safe distance. She didn't want anyone to realize she was with Avant and Toya, but made sure to stay close enough to handle the business if something went down. Right now, her main focus was on the man standing among the crowd watching Avant.

Her phone pinged. Tyler's text said *I recognize one of the people who made contact with Avant from our person of interest list. I would do a little more digging to see if there are any connections to the people in the outlier group they were looking into.*

Toya ran up to her and hugged her after she finished exploring one of the exhibits called the Climbing Schooner. "Did you see me?"

"Yes." Mia ruffled the perfectly formed afro puffs. At least Toya had waited until they were about to leave the museum to approach. "So what's next?"

Toya looked back as Avant made his way over. "The Ferris wheel."

Avant moved forward until he stood next to Mia. "Then she wants to pick up some taffy apples on the way out."

"And cinnamon almonds and Garrett's popcorn," Toya added with a mile-wide grin.

Emily returned from the restroom. "Are you ready?"

Mia switched on the drone that had been hovering over Avant most of the day. Now it was set to follow her since she would be walking with them. She'd review the footage on her phone.

Toya frowned in answer to Emily's question. "If it means we have time for pizza and game night before you go."

Mia couldn't help but smile as she glanced at her watch. "I wish I could, but I have dinner plans with my fiancée today."

"Can't you invite him to have pizza with us?" Toya looked at Avant whose face instantly formed into a neutral expression.

Avant shrugged. "That's up to Mia."

"Let's get to it. Maybe we can play Uno so I can get my championship title back," Toya said, wiggling her eyebrows.

Avant gave her shoulder a gentle pat. "You won't get that title back tonight."

Mia's mind flitted to a few major questions. What would having a family look like with Calvin? Would she be a single parent within a marriage? Would Calvin continue to make time to balance his life? Or would the next project have him back in workaholic mode?

Frustration set in as she returned to the fact that he'd already made a decision that delayed them having a family. Mia thought about Toya's invite and texted that Calvin should join them for pizza. She wanted to see how he was with the little girl that had been under her watch.

* * *

Mia moved toward the hostess stand in the Giordano's near the expressway on Halsted. Since the encounter with Gabriel, Calvin didn't drive himself to The Castle anymore. Tonight, his security detail, most likely Nicco, would drop him off at the restaurant, and she'd be responsible for getting him home safely.

Avant and Toya entered a few minutes later since they drove in separate vehicles. Thankfully, Emily had gone home, and all that pawing had ended for the day.

"Everything okay?" Mia asked, studying Avant's frowning face.

"Yeah, just thinking about the odd conversation at Navy Pier about children's workbooks." Avant reached out to take Toya's hand before she bounced off without them.

"Can we get pepperoni on the pizza?" Toya's gaze tracked the deep-dish pizza being delivered to a table of college students.

"Sure." Mia smiled, following the hostess past the students to their booth.

They were having appetizers when Calvin's call came in. "Are you on your way?"

"We were delayed by an accident," Calvin explained. "Go ahead and eat. Just save me a slice."

"Okay." Mia ended the call. "Calvin's running late. Hopefully he'll make it by the time the pizza arrives."

"Avant, do you think mom will let me stay with you again? I'm having fun. Except for the homework stuff," Toya said, grabbing the last mozzarella wedge.

"We'll have to see. I'll be traveling a lot over the next few months, but the three of us can hang out after that." Avant smiled as the waiter arrived, placed the deep dish on the silver stand, and served the first slices.

"Mia too?" Toya attempted to lift the thick pizza slice to take a bite.

"We'll have to see what her schedule looks like." Avant unwrapped his fork and knife and sliced into the gooey cheese. "Speaking of schedules … will you be with us for the remainder of the week?"

Mia didn't know that answer. She'd have to follow up with Daron. "We'll see."

Toya kept them entertained by retelling how much fun she'd had since coming to Chicago. Calvin slipped into the restaurant as they were having dessert.

"Sorry, I'm late." He kissed Mia on the cheek before sliding into the space next to her. "Nice seeing you again."

Avant slid a plate toward Calvin, grinning as he said, "As you see, I did manage to leave you a slice. Mia's request."

Calvin glanced down at the pizza, looked up at Avant and said. "You have it. Didn't mean to put you through too much trouble. I'll just order something to go." He took Mia's hand in his. "One slice has never been enough."

"Toya, this is Calvin," Mia said, glaring at Calvin. Toya plopped a piece of chocolate chip cookie into her mouth, oblivious to the tension at the table.

The waiter returned to see if Calvin wanted anything to drink. Calvin declined but ordered chicken alfredo and a salad to go. They made small talk, with Toya asking Calvin a lot of questions about his profession as he ignored that slice of pizza, and Avant as well.

"I need to get her home, Avant said finally, miffed at being left out of the conversation. He stood and grabbed the bill.

"I'll walk them out while you wait for your food." Mia nudged Calvin to let her out of the booth.

"I'll be a couple of steps behind you," Calvin said, whipping out his wallet to cover their portion of the meal.

"Oh, I don't need an entourage," Avant teased. "Mia can handle things just fine."

"I'm sure she can," Calvin shot back. "It's not her I'm worried about."

Mia followed Avant and Toya to the car. Her eye caught three suspicious men working their way through the parking lot scanning the vehicles. Mia waved to Avant as he pulled out. She stepped back and extracted the key fob from her purse. She watched for a moment to see if the men followed her friend. They didn't, which left only one other possible target.

She pulled Calvin to her side the moment he stepped out the door and rushed him to the car. One of the guys saw Calvin and tapped the other man on the shoulder, gesturing toward Mia.

"What?"

"Something's not right," Mia whispered watching as the men wove between several cars trying to make it to where they stood. She hurried Calvin into the car. Mia pulled out of the parking lot as the men hopped into a dark blue sedan.

Chapter 20

"Where are you going?" Calvin said as she headed north instead of south towards home.

"Just checking to see if I'm being paranoid." Mia glanced in the rearview mirror and noticed the sedan gaining on her.

Calvin followed her line of sight. "But you're not."

"They were looking for a car, which meant they couldn't possibly be there for you." Before leaving Navy Pier they had checked Avant's Volvo for a tracker. She hadn't found one. "Maybe they were looking for Avant."

"Why would they be looking for him?" Calvin asked, his lips forming a thin line.

Mia relaxed a little as she put some distance between them and a few cars moved into the lanes. "Have you received any threats?"

"No."

"Have you heard from Gabriel?" Mia hated that he was still on the loose. There was always the chance he would retaliate for being shut down in Lake Geneva. Money was a great motivator, but for Gabriel to go this far meant someone else was pulling the strings.

"Nothing from him." Calvin retrieved his phone from his pocket. "Maybe we should call Daron."

"I'm trained to handle this." Her knuckles turned white from gripping the steering wheel. The sedan made an attempt to slide in behind her. She slowed down so she remained between a Buick SUV and an eighteen-wheeler, so he couldn't get in. With traffic so thick, this wasn't going to be a quick getaway.

"We have company," she said.

The sedan managed to wedge itself in between her and the BMW that pulled up behind her. She took the opportunity to move into the right-hand lane and with a quick acceleration, worked her way off at the next exit. The sedan wasn't able to make the off-ramp in time.

She whipped up the ramp, ran through the lights, and entered the on ramp heading back south.

Inwardly she berated herself. Maybe Cameron was right. She *was* off her game. She hadn't even noticed when those guys had pulled up at the restaurant. "We need to stay at a motel for a few hours until we know it's safe to return home."

* * *

A little over an hour later, she pulled into a nondescript motel and stashed their vehicle in the back parking lot.

"Ask for a room on the rear side, one night. Don't give them your real name. Pay cash," she said as he opened the door. "Don't worry. They won't ask for ID."

Calvin walked down the concrete path leading to the glass doors of the lobby. Mia followed with one hand within close reach of a weapon. She stopped at the corner of the building, watching him enter the office. She kept her gaze going between the mild traffic, the road, and him. She tried to put together the pieces of what was going on. Avant and Calvin didn't look anything alike, so it couldn't be a case of mistaken identity.

Minutes later, they entered the room as two drunk men argued outside several feet from their window.

Calvin left the gap in the curtain where anyone looking in could only see the foot of the bed. "I haven't been in a motel like this since college."

"I bet you thought you left those days behind," Mia teased as she texted Avant to make sure they'd made it home safely.

"Actually, this one isn't so bad. At least it's clean, despite the bad drapes." Calvin dropped down on the bed. His gaze narrowed on her in that same way he did when she performed her daily ground sweeps, security protocols, and updates. "You're sure this is safer than being at home?"

"For now, we'll watch the security cameras at home to make sure we don't have company for the next couple of hours. If not, we'll go home." Mia wanted to send someone to check out Avant's Volvo again. Calvin may not have been the original target. She shook off the feelings of guilt. "I checked the car for a tracker and didn't find one."

Calvin loosened his tie and pulled out his phone. "This kind of reminds me of the hotel on that back road in Louisiana. The one on the way to your grandma's house."

"It does." Mia looked at Calvin and realized that last week they hadn't really been communicating well. She peered at the security feed of their home on his phone and saw nothing out of the norm. "When are you expected to go to Durabia?"

"It's tentatively scheduled to start within six months." Calvin patted the mattress next to him. "Would you consider coming with me if I have Daron arrange housing in the Free Zone?"

"That doesn't fix the problem." Mia lowered herself onto the thin foam mattress. "Just because five people can get away with breaking the law doesn't mean the sixth person will have the same experience. We can't assume because other people have done it then we won't have any problems."

"We have the palace on our side. The Kings are related to the Royals"

Mia frowned, thinking about the recent change in leadership in Durabia. "They're on your side now, but not everyone is happy about how they're running things. Kamran being with Ellena has brought out some serious issues from the old guard. Not to mention the fact that she took down a reigning sheikh of a country that was established long before Durabia ever was a drop on the map."

"She had every right to do what she did," Calvin shot back. He was well aware that Ellena had two major strikes against her—being a western woman living in a Middle Eastern world and marrying royalty put her squarely in the center of the drama. "No one can fault her actions."

"But the fact that she had to do those things to gain her freedom is what concerns me," she countered. "Just because they're not making noise doesn't mean they aren't making moves. And the fact that you're all set to help Durabia with its military defense puts a target squarely on your back as well."

Calvin inhaled deeply. "Unfortunately, being a target comes with my job."

Mia popped off the bed, heading to the bathroom. She could feel the tears building in her eyes. The fact was, she wasn't ready to lose another person she loved. Despite all the strides they had made, Calvin was drifting all over again.

Chapter 21

Calvin felt the heat of Vikkas' stare. The only difference between his physical appearance and his twin, Jai, was the shock of silver at the widow's peak of his dark, silky hair. The olive complexions slightly matched Dro, who unlike them, had Latino heritage instead of East Indian. The Kings, all from various ethnic backgrounds and belief systems, had always been formidable when handling an issue, but realizing he was now the issue at hand was a problem.

He stood in the state-of-the-art command center of The Castle giving all nine of the Kings an update on the Durabian shield. "You do understand the importance of this project?"

"And to your family. Yes." Calvin couldn't keep the irritation out of his tone. Once again, the Kings were questioning his ability to execute because of the Gabriel situation. Even now the man was still giving him grief.

"Do we have a problem?" Dro asked, peering at Shaz who took a bite out of the jerk chicken he'd had catered in, along with a full spread from Ms. Mabel's Jamaican Joint. Calvin would love to wrap his appetite around those good-smelling morsels, but right now the Kings were having him wrap their minds around the shield's capabilities. An edge existed among a few of the men, and it was high time he laid that out in the open.

"Clearly you have an issue with me," he said, scanning the faces of the men. "Lay it out instead of giving me attitude and interrupting my presentation on the challenges that this concept will face."

As the project progressed closer to the development stage, Calvin realized that the shield would also need a detection system. A totally different aspect that he didn't believe was considered in the timeline development.

"Meeting with Gabriel put you on people's radar," Shaz added, before sliding some of the plantains off the serving dish in front of him. "It makes it much more difficult for you to discreetly work on the Durabia protective shield here."

"Are you going to save any for the rest of us?" Calvin asked.

"Now there's a classic question," Grant, the architect with the brooding look, mumbled.

Shaz froze, then looked over to Calvin. "Oh, you wanted some, too?"

"Don't worry, we have always ordered a second stash, because the man's appetite is legendary." Daron pulled up images of Gabriel meeting with several groups of men, ones Calvin didn't recognize.

"We need you to head to Durabia ASAP," Vikkas said, finally sliding a plate Calvin's way.

Dwayne, the educator of the group, looked at Calvin. "Is that something you'll be able to do?"

Mia flashed in his mind. Calvin felt it was better for his relationship if he could stick to the original schedule. "It's not ideal but—"

"Now, if you don't think you can handle it," Jai said, glancing over at Vikkas who grimaced at that veiled strong-arm tactic, then to Calvin. "Let us know now so we can make a different assessment of what needs to be done."

"Guys, give Calvin a day to think about it." Daron held up his hand to ward off any more pressure coming from anyone else. "We'll work out an alternate plan in the meantime."

The Kings finished off the meal, and there was no more talk of the project. The conversation drifted to more pleasant topics—the women in their lives, how they came to be Kings, and even some of their personal goals. Calvin still didn't feel as comfortable opening up to them. At least, they made good on the assertion of a personal stash. It had been hidden behind the fully-stocked bar.

About an hour later, each one of them slowly made their way from the room. This time, none of them looked his way. Not a good sign. Calvin lingered, waiting for Daron to follow them out.

Instead of leaving, he motioned for Calvin to take a seat. "Do you have a problem with Vikkas, or the project?"

"I have a problem with him coming at me as if I'm a child."

"Look, you may have overreacted to Vikkas' comment because of everything that's happened with your parents, Gabriel, and Mia. You have to consider The Castle a blended family." Daron perched on the edge of the conference table. "If this is to work, you have to respect and embrace the differences and deal with them accordingly."

Calvin gathered up his notebook and stuck it in his bag. "I'm committed to this project, even though it's already having a negative effect on my life." He locked gazes with Daron. "I didn't appreciate being treated like I don't understand the impact of what I'm doing."

"I understand." Daron stood, grabbing his materials. "Take some time to reconnect with Mia. We both know that you need to be in Durabia in the next couple of days. You've done quite a bit of the initial work already, and the next steps really need to happen there."

Calvin followed him out of the boardroom. "I wanted more time to convince Mia to come with me."

"She has valid points," Daron said, as he locked up the room. "You have to remember she recently lost a good friend, which probably has her in a 'life is short' state of mind. Now, because of this project, you're asking her to rush a marriage, delay having a family, and move overseas."

Calvin thought how relaxed Mia was with Avant and Toya at Giordano's the other night. "Reconnecting with Avant couldn't have come at a worse time."

Even though Avant was leaving town soon, Calvin didn't want his mishandling of this Durabia project to push her into his arms. Those two seemed to have a chemistry that felt … solid.

"He may be playing a factor in it, but you need to find out what's going on in Mia's head if you want to find a win-win scenario." Daron led Calvin back into his private office in the Morgan Park wing of the Castle. Each King had a wing that was named for the area where they had grown up. "I can assign Mia to be on your protection detail, which could force her to go to Durabia or quit Crossroads Security." He set his bag down on the steel cabinet that lined the wall. "But that isn't going to solve your personal problems. It will just keep her in close proximity. You'll have to do the rest."

Calvin shook his head. "I don't want her to be forced to do anything. She loves working for you. I don't want to put her in the position to have to make that kind of decision." Calvin leaned on the back of the chair that faced the desk. "Can we push my departure back a month?"

Daron focused on him for a long while. "You need to figure out whether you're ready for the sacrifices that being a Knight requires, which could mean trying to maintain a long-distance relationship with Mia. We can't help you manage your love life. Trust me, we've had our own challenges." He stood, rounded the desk and lowered himself into the executive chair. "If you continue with this project, you'll be on the plane in forty-eight hours heading to Durabia."

Chapter 22

Mia was in the kitchen when he arrived home. The rich smell of gumbo filled the air. Calvin's stomach growled because that good stuff wasn't on its way down to his belly. He was feeling more like Shaz— he'd had a full meal, but the scent of what she was cooking made him hungry all over again.

"Rough day?" Mia looked up, smiling.

He kissed her on the cheek. "Today had me reevaluating what I want."

She pulled out two bowls from the cabinet before filling them with some of that rich, savory Southern concoction that made his mouth water. "How so?"

Calvin carried them to the table. "I thought I wanted to be a Knight of the Castle working to make a difference in the world."

He wanted to be a part of a team. Not to be treated like an adolescent who couldn't get his act together. He had to admit Daron might be right, he was a little sensitive to Vikkas' comment. Both because of the negative effect this project had already had on his family, and how it reminded him of the snide comments made throughout his schooling. He spent years enduring the privileged students belittling his intelligence and treating him like he didn't belong. He had no desire to be a part of that again.

Mia joined him with two glasses of Green River and slices of cornbread to accompany the good stuff. "You've always looked at the desired outcome without taking in all the challenges that come along with it."

She did have a point. He had always been a "finish line" kind of guy. "They want me to leave for Durabia in forty-eight hours." Calvin watched Mia's face for a reaction. None was forthcoming.

"I see." Mia crumbled some cornbread into her gumbo. "And you don't want to go."

"Not without you." Calvin reached for her hand. "I assumed that since you'd been before, you'd have no problem going when I said yes. That was my mistake."

"Thank you for acknowledging that. However, while a long-distance relationship is not ideal, maybe we can do it. I'll make arrangements to see you at least once a month." Mia patted his hand knowing it wasn't the answer he was hoping for. "We'll go from there."

Calvin extracted his hand and scooped up a spoonful of gumbo into his mouth. "I honestly took coming home to our nightly talks over dinner and our other activities for granted. Until now. My decision to take on this project is forcing us to give up everything we built here."

He now had a permanent protection team. One watched the house, and the other was responsible for getting him to the Castle safely. Little things like making a pit stop on the way home weren't so simple. However, great accomplishments were rarely achieved without sacrifice and challenges.

"Pack your bags and get ready to go, but use the full forty-eight hours to decide how you want to proceed." Mia pushed her chair back and rounded the table, sliding into his lap and winding her arms around his neck. "While I'm not a fan of living in Durabia, I'll support you in whatever you decide. I may complain a lot, but I'll always support you."

"I love you, Mia Jakob, soon to be Atwood." Calvin gazed into her eyes, then brought his lips to kiss her before pulling away to say, "And thank you."

Mia intensified the kiss as she straddled him. "I'm going to need you to thank me … properly."

Calvin shifted the chair back and lifted her. She wrapped her legs around him as he carried her up the stairs to the bedroom. He laid her on the paisley comforter.

Calvin pulled the t-shirt over her head, revealing a sheer teal bra. "So beautiful."

He lovingly caressed each breast, flickering his tongue over her nipples as he removed her bra. Working his way down, he slipped off the remainder of her clothes. He parted her thighs, working several fingers into her center until her body shook with a tremor of orgasm.

"You have too many clothes on." Mia removed his shirt. Her fingers traced his muscles, delivering sensual kisses along his collarbone and down his pecs. She wrapped a leg around his back pulling his body closer, grinding against his growing erection.

Calvin's lips made a trail from her breast down her torso. Mia moaned as his tongue swirled and twirled at her core. She gripped his shoulders as her body quivered. Calvin held her hips, and lavished her pearl with love until she lost complete control of her body.

He sheathed himself in that welcome heat by entering her in one thrust. Mia slowly began rocking and rotating her hips. Exhilarating him with the heat rolling off her through each stroke. The way Mia rode him this time was different. As though she was draining him of every ounce of energy. As if there wouldn't be another time. She kissed him with such passion that he felt like he was drowning in an abyss of pleasure. Calvin's soul trembled the moment Mia stared into his eyes—hard, thorough. Their love making was like nothing he'd ever experienced, exquisite, intense, and slightly scary.

Calvin's heart hammered against his chest as Mia's body collapsed onto his. They stayed that way—almost forever.

"I'm not going to Durabia." Calvin held her close, sliding a hand through her long wavy hair. "At least not right now."

Mia slid her hand across his abs. "Are you really not going?"

"I'm choosing us." Calvin felt confident in his decision. "We need more time before I go."

Mia studied his face as if looking for any trace of doubt. "You're sure about this?"

"I'll focus on selling several inventions I have in my arsenal that would build and increase our family's generational wealth." Calvin's hand gently stroked her arm. "Daron's team has everything he needs to continue work on the shield. I can consult via video conference."

She leaned back from his chest, staring into his eyes. "Are Daron and the Kings going to be satisfied with that?"

"They're going to have to be." He planted a kiss on her forehead. "I have no plans to be on a plane in the next forty-eight hours."

Chapter 23

A couple of weeks had passed and Mia didn't know how she let Daron and Cameron convince her to talk Calvin into going to Durabia. He'd been in the Middle East for two weeks. She'd planned to visit him for a week, but Daron and Cameron had also persuaded her to agree to stay an entire month.

"Calvin, you should go."

"Why? What changed?" He stared deeply into her eyes then tightened his lips. "It was Daron, wasn't it?"

"No, actually, it was Cameron." She grabbed his hand. "I love that you were willing to stay but it won't maintain our lives. All we would be are lions passing in the jungle."

"I don't agree." Calvin gave her a peck. "Sweetheart..."

Mia put an index finger of his full lips. "You will be working on Durabia time, which is what? Nine hours ahead of us."

Calvin moved her index finger away from his lips and studied her face. "I appreciate this change. I'm not going without you."

"I plan to come in a few weeks and stay awhile. If it's not working, we can always revert to Plan A." Mia grabbed his luggage that was near the hall closet, then handed it to him. "You have a plane to catch."

"You're sure?"

She nodded.

Calvin kissed her passionately. "I miss you already."

He didn't make that flight. Instead, he stayed and made sure to say a "proper" goodbye.

Mentally, Mia was already planning her trip back home, and she hadn't even left for Durabia yet. She was glad she had a few more weeks to embrace her new norm to support him before kissing it goodbye. Calvin would be surprised when he realized that she'd be there for an extended period.

Technically, she'd be working for Daron, but having to conform to the customs of Durabia changed the team dynamics unless they were doing something under the cover of night. The frustrating part was the cultural differences of the Middle East meant that joining him there would still keep them apart. She would still miss him the same—or even more—than if they were at home.

Her cell vibrated, jarring her out of her thoughts.

"Hey Avant." Mia had only talked to him a couple of times since he left Chicago. And it was for the best. She had to put her focus on the relationship that mattered.

"I'm in Chicago for a day. Probably the last time for a while." Avant's voice became muffled. "I need to go, but are you free to meet for a drink or dinner later?"

"Text me the info." Mia disconnected as Cameron entered the smoothie bar giving her a probing look.

Cameron was definitely ready for their workout, wearing all black with her hair pulled back in a ponytail and a towel thrown over her shoulder.

"What?" Mia asked.

Cameron smirked. "Was that Avant?"

"Why do you ask that?" Mia slid the phone into her duffle bag. "It could have been Calvin."

Cameron claimed a seat next to her at the bar. "That particular look in your eye has only been reserved for Avant."

What the hell did that mean? "My dad asked me some questions that had me thinking. Can I live the rest of my life dealing with Calvin's flaws? The last few months I've been leaning toward no," Mia confessed, which had been a hard pill to swallow.

"How much does Avant have to do with that?" Cameron waved off the approaching smoothie attendant.

Mia grabbed the gym bag. She needed this workout. "A little. It has more to do with me wanting to have kids. Calvin taking on this Durabia project is just another reminder that family is too far in the future with him."

Cameron stood and headed into the public area of the gym. "What did your counselor say about your sudden change of heart on marriage?"

Mia hadn't made an appointment with a grief professional. For the most part she was fine, with the exception of moments that sparked memories. She followed Cameron through the weight area, passing the treadmill until they reached the corridor leading to a private room.

"Remember, being a good friend and being a good mate are two different things." Cameron stepped on the treadmill. "Things roll off you as a friend that affect you differently as the significant other. There's a period of transition between the two roles."

Mia sat the gym bag on the floor and got on the machine next to Cameron. "I'm not planning on breaking off my engagement with Calvin and running off to marry Avant."

Cameron lifted a perfectly arched eyebrow. "I wasn't suggesting that. I was simply saying look at things realistically before you set your life on fire."

"I'm not trying to burn my life down," Mia said, pressing the button to increase the incline.

"Being with Avant makes you feel closer to Diana, who was supposed to be your maid of honor." She hopped off the machine and grabbed two water bottles from the fridge. "There's a lot of emotions at play that you're either not ready to acknowledge or are still buried deep."

Mia suddenly felt overcome with emotion. Cameron turned on some

House music and handed over a water bottle, then changed the subject, effectively letting Mia off the hook.

The one thing Mia liked about Cameron was that she never pushed too much. Unlike Calvin's mother who'd been calling quite often.

* * *

The restaurant was crowded when Mia reached Avant at the bar. She tried to ignore the two men Daron assigned to shadow her as they slid into the empty stools at the end of the bar, facing the door.

Mia tapped Avant on his shoulder. "Hey handsome."

He stood, giving her a hug before moving his suit jacket off the seat next to him. Mia smiled as he slid a sloe gin fizz in front of her.

"Have you talked with Toya recently?" Mia missed the little girl's energy and their game nights.

"Yeah, I convinced Leticia and a few other cousins we need a trip to Disneyland when I come back to the States. Toya was excited."

"That's good."

"I've got to do a better job of checking on Leticia." Avant stared at her left hand. "Is there something going on with you and Calvin?"

"Why do you ask?" Mia sipped her sloe gin fizz, wondering at the sudden hopeful tone in his voice.

"You're not wearing your engagement ring."

She glanced down at her bare finger then back up at him. "I took it off at the gym and forgot to put in back on."

His eyes drilled into hers, trying to determine a deeper meaning behind the slipup.

Mia moved her hands to her lap. "I meant to ask you what happened with the client your boss didn't intend for you to take."

"We declined to take him on as a full-time client." Avant grabbed his drink as the little black box on the counter vibrated and flashed red, signaling their table was ready.

Mia followed suit. "Did your boss ever say why?"

Avant's hand rested on the small of her back as he guided her toward the host stand. "The owner is being investigated for questionable practices in another one of his companies."

"I can see why he would want to steer clear." Mia couldn't shake the feeling that there was more to the story. The person who made contact with Avant at Navy Pier had simply asked questions about a children's workbook. "Umm, where *did* you get Toya's workbooks?"

"Leticia sent them with her." Avant slid in the booth across from her. "I had to help Toya with some of the questions, since parts of it were really too advanced for a ten-year-old."

"How so?"

"The problems started on her level, but she was to use her answer to calculate the next one which was really too large and complex."

"Why didn't you just skip it?" Mia scanned the crowd to make sure there were no questionable characters nearby.

"The answer created a code that she needed for the next set of problems." He picked up the menu and glanced at the selections, frowning. "Are you looking for children's workbooks already?"

"I'm quitting my day job to create children's activity books." Mia laughed, but then a thought hit her where she wondered if they were using Avant to unknowingly pass along information. Something about the situation nagged at her. Like she was missing a key piece that would make things clearer. Her fingers were crossed that she was simply being paranoid, and Avant wasn't actually still being targeted.

Chapter 24

An entire month of not coming home to Mia had Calvin putting his all into the work. He didn't want this to become a permanent situation. Trying to stay focused while wondering how much time she was spending with that "high school friend" put a damper on the wonderful time he should be having in such an awesome place. Avant had subtly changed his schedule to work from home to reconnect with her. So, it wasn't unreasonable to think he would extend his stay in Chicago to do more of the same.

"Mia will be here next week," Daron said as though sensing what had Calvin so preoccupied.

"I'm looking forward to being in the same room with her. This video conferencing is torture."

Calvin grabbed the gear bag. Today they were visiting the potential launch spots around Durabia. Getting info on the tallest building in the city would set a major point. The Range Rover pulled in the driveway in front of the hotel which was their first testing spot.

Calvin should've asked more questions about the project going in. He didn't expect the nearby countries, with the exception of the one he'd researched, to be against Durabia and a potential threat. Having more communities close and willing to attack changed the response time.

"Can those lines in your forehead get any deeper?" Daron asked.

"Are they willing to create new monuments that could technically be considered a tourist attraction?" Calvin glanced over his notes. "But in reality, it will be one of the permanent anchors in the shield?"

"Possibly." Daron keyed something into his tablet. "How long do you think this will take?"

"Honestly, phase one may take a year for the build to be completely done. The other concept will take longer."

Daron's head whipped to him. "What concept are we talking about?"

"The liquid concept is temporary until the team is finished building the prototype." Calvin had developed the two liquids combined to create a layer similar to a mask on a protective suit. He modified The Arabians, hovercrafts that looked like a cross between a jet ski and motorcycle, for the project. They could be ridden or controlled by remote. He adapted The Arabians to catch any drippings and work to break down the material when it was time. "We want each layer to be sheer so it will take more time, but when we get to the materials required to provide protection from bombs, that will become more of a challenge."

"What about if it isn't working properly?" Daron asked. "I want to get possible scenarios to the detection system development team."

"It wouldn't be a problem. We can launch a working Arabian to the needed location," Calvin said, then went on to explain that the first layer was for chemical attacks, but there were multiple sheers within that layer to attempt to battle anything, whether it was a nerve, blister, choking, or blood agent. "We get in trouble if there's an issue with the first ones."

"We have teams heading up to the 125th and 148th floors." Daron glanced out of the window in the direction of the entrance and the men who were situated there. "In order not to draw too much attention we can only have two test launches of The Arabians."

Calvin handed Daron one of the two wrist remotes, then strapped his on under a bracelet. The Arabians were in temporary storage containers nearby. They needed to see how quickly they could get in position with the material to keep the liquid from dripping on the city. It would be launched seconds after the liquid was released.

"How do you go so long without seeing Cameron?" Calvin asked, pulling out Daron's tablet to stream images from the drones recording the dry run.

"We get creative to make it work, talk daily. Have virtual meals together." Daron checked his devices. "Cameron's schedule is flexible. She comes to visit me and stays at least a week if I can't make it back to the States."

"I'll have to find out more about those virtual meals," he said as they received the notification that the teams were in place.

Daron stepped out of the vehicle and he followed suit. "Your com is on," he said, tapping his ear before heading off in the opposite direction. Meaning no more private conversation for a while.

Calvin hit the corner of the building where he could have a sight line to the side. "All right. Ready to launch in three, two, one."

"Mine is up," Daron confirmed.

"Already have a problem. Someone is blocking the unit with a car. It can't get out. We definitely need to use the unit to release from the top." Calvin watched as the blocking vehicle finally moved, giving clear access. "Launching now."

The second testing went off without any issues.

Daron met him back at the Range Rover. "I'll head to the next location since it's farther away than yours."

"Will the earpieces work from that distance?" Calvin glanced at the tablet to make sure The Arabian was firmly back in the container. He made a note to switch out the storage unit before the next test. In the second location, they were going to test how well several Arabians would connect, since one unit wasn't enough to blanket the city.

"Yes. Wait for the two teams to return before you head to the next location." Daron scanned the area as though looking for trouble. "Rumor is there's a group that's very interested in what you're doing. I'm digging more into it, but we need to take extra precautions until I'm able to track them down."

Daron tapped on the Range Rover's window before heading to the other vehicle. Calvin placed the controller back into the bag. "I'm going to run to the restroom before we head out."

Roc, a beefier version of Calvin, stepped out of the passenger seat. "I'll go with you."

Calvin hated this part of what he did. The guards. The only time he didn't mind so much was when he was under the discreet protection of Mia. The time Daron's company stationed her in a security assignment where she pretended to be his wife was the best thing to ever happen to him. He was sure she was his forever. He hoped and prayed she still felt that way about him.

Roc entered the restroom first, then came out a few moments later. "You're good."

Calvin brushed past him and still did his own sweep of the area, given Daron's recent admission and the fact that Mia had taught him to trust only himself. *Mia, my love, what are you up to right now?*

When he moved from the restroom back into the lobby, he asked, "Has the team made it down from the upper floors?"

"Yes," Roc answered.

"Mr. Atwood, could I speak to you for a moment?" A familiar voice called from across the lobby.

Calvin turned and was unsettled to see Gabriel leaving the side of a man wearing a white dishdasha—tunic—before he approached.

"Sorry, I don't have time."

"I'd hoped you'd see the error of your ways and change your mind." Gabriel tried to maneuver around Roc to get in front of Calvin. "But there are several people interested in why you're in Durabia. I'd hate for you to get yourself ... killed."

Calvin tugged at his shirt material to made sure his sleeve was covering the device on his forearm. "Is that a threat?"

Roc stepped closer, saying softly into his communication device, "We may have a situation."

He held up a hand to stave off Roc, who didn't look happy about the command.

"I'm just reminding you that your higher moral compass isn't going to fill your bank account the way I can. And if you're going to risk life and limb, you might as well be compensated well for it." Gabriel smirked, waving Mohammad Omar over. A man whose dossier was placed in Calvin's files when he first arrived. "I can make that happen."

"Actually, I can make that happen without you." Calvin shifted forward to move around him again. "So why would I align myself with someone who is only interested in the highest bidder."

"Mohammad would like to speak to you about the project you're working on." Despite Roc's best efforts, Gabriel blocked Calvin's path to the door as Mohammad approached.

The only thing Calvin knew about Mohammad was that he was from Nadaum. The same country of the ruler that Sheikha Ellena Khan had destroyed. The family of that man was now gunning for Kamran Ali Khan, the current ruling Sheikh of Durabia. This was the reason Calvin had been commissioned to create the protective shield. Going to war and having thousands of casualties was something Sheikh Kamran wanted to prevent. Durabia was unlike other Middle Eastern countries in that regard. Peace was their main objective. Kind of hard to maintain when a woman, an American, had caused a major uproar in every major Middle Eastern country in the area.

Now with this little ambush, he had to wonder if Gabriel was referring to the protection pods or Durabia's top secret protective shields. How much intel did he have?

"I understand that you're a busy man, but I would like to schedule some time to discuss how we could work together." Mohammad snapped his fingers and one of the men hovering nearby slid something into his hand. He extended a metal business card with gold wording and studded with diamonds. "It was a pleasure meeting you."

Mohammad swept past them and ambled toward a group of men with ominous expressions, who were glaring a hole in Calvin.

"Atwood," Gabriel sneered as he walked away.

Roc pulled a box from his jacket, then plucked the card from Calvin's hand and dropped it inside. "You're not about to get me in trouble with Daron."

"What is that?" Calvin glanced at the box as they moved toward the door.

"If there's a tracker embedded in the card, this container will block the signal." Roc held the door for Calvin, sweeping an eagle-eyed gaze over the area behind them. "We'll scan it once we return to the palace then give it back to you if Daron says it's safe."

While Daron didn't have to go too far to track down the rumor anymore, Calvin didn't like that Gabriel was there so close to Mia arriving. Damn, he wished he'd given the green light to Cameron to shut him down her way instead of trying to have Daron's team handle things legally.

Chapter 25

Mia was way past agitated. Somehow, being in the Middle East made her feel like she'd lost her independence. She could go into the city or the mall, but the majority of her life was neatly nestled inside of Calvin's world and project. She didn't really have a life of her own. During the two weeks she'd been there, she couldn't deny that Calvin was trying to make every effort to keep their relationship thriving. The impromptu dates and overnight stays at private upscale hotels had been great. She found it interesting that in the states she tried her best to uphold the law, but in the Middle East she was breaking the law every time she and Calvin shared a bed. That did not sit well with her, and it was not something easily forgotten.

Her phone vibrated, and Cameron's name appeared on the screen. Mia took one last look at the breathtaking water feature below her balcony. She slid the glass door closed behind her as she reentered the luxurious bedroom of the Jamillah Hotel; one that Calvin took great pains to ensure would shower her in luxury.

"Hey what's up?" Mia asked as she grabbed her gear off the cream couch situated in a room that was fit for a queen.

She hated that she couldn't carry a real gun. She didn't want to be shooting tranquilizer bullets at people who were shooting real ones in her direction. Daron had done it for her protection. Most of his main team who carried weapons signed on to take the risk and the complications of being involved in a shooting. Since she was engaged to Calvin, they wanted to make sure she didn't run into any problems that would draw attention to the project. Daron was aware that someone within the walls of Durabia had to be talking if other governments were aware of the shield and its purpose. His original deadline had just been moved and that meant less time with Calvin.

"Calling to let you know Avant popped up on Tyler's radar again." Cameron's tone was more serious than expected. "Some shady characters are looking into him."

"Last time I spoke with him, he was heading overseas. He didn't say exactly where," Mia said. "Hopefully, it will give me time to look into it before he takes that vacation with Toya and Leticia." Mia felt a little guilty keeping in touch with Avant, knowing that he wanted to be more than friends. But things would have to take a drastic turn for her to leave Calvin for him. Hopefully, at some point Avant would get that memo.

"How are you and Calvin handling Durabian life?"

Her bare feet sank into the plush fabric of the cream and gold rug as she grabbed several knives from the coffee table. The knives were made with special alloys that would not set off metal detectors. Daron's way of compensating for not having her weapon of choice. "It's been an interesting and enlightening experience."

"Have you taken the time to decide if Calvin is still your forever after?"

"Dr. Stone, I've been doing *a lot* of reflecting." Mia attached the knives to her body then scanned the room to make sure she had everything she needed, then sent Cameron a video call request via the special communication app Daron created.

When Cameron accepted and the call switched over, she said, "Many people don't believe just friends with the opposite sex is possible. In your case, we know Avant wants more." Cameron appeared on Mia's phone wearing a dark grey leather jacket and matching jeans. "The question is, do you? Because you have to be clear if you want both him *and* Calvin in your life."

Mia tried to sweep past that verbal bullet by focusing on the fact that she was glad Cameron was heading to Durabia. The way Cameron was dressed reminded Mia that the weather was cooling down in the States. Technically, so was Durabia's. Earlier, the heat was scorching, and people aimed to make it straight to their destinations instead of taking in more of the sights along the way. Now that the weather had cooled, more people were out and about, taking their time to enjoy the mall, the water show and so many other places Durabia had to offer.

Mia slipped into her shoes, mulling over Cameron's words. "Calvin will definitely have a problem with that."

"He will if you don't make him feel secure in his position in your life. I know a woman who told her husband to stop seeing his best female friend." Cameron shifted the luggage on the ottoman in front of her bed and took a seat. "He secretly maintained contact with her through the years, only calling her from work, seeing her over lunch. If he wanted to cheat with her, he could have, and the wife would have been none the wiser. But had she found out ..."

"I understand." Mia wasn't ready to have that conversation with Calvin yet. "Being here has given me time to think. I've had a couple of virtual grief counseling sessions which helped put things in perspective."

"Good."

"It's great you're coming. I'm getting a little homesick." Mia looked at the time on the wall clock. "Work calls. I'll see you when you make it into town."

She put on a hijab to cover her hair and shoulders, which she only had to wear within the palace grounds, then walked out of the room heading to the helicopter. She only smiled as she neared Calvin making sure not to touch him. "Good morning. How did you sleep?"

"Not as well as I would have if you were by my side," Calvin said snapping a controller on his forearm.

"We're just doing testing today, correct?" Mia accepted the tablet Calvin handed her.

"I need you to record the times and monitor the camera." Calvin angled so that he faced her head on. "This is the first attempt with the liquid layer, but in testing we had trouble with The Arabians connecting after the shield is deployed."

Mia secured herself in the helicopter as they rose. She watched, amazed, as the first layer of the shield came up. Calvin couldn't have come up with this shield idea in a few months. She realized that she had to accept the part she played in the distance with Calvin. She had been going through the motions, pretending to be okay after Diana died. Maybe coming to Durabia was good for her, since it forced her to face the issue that she'd been avoiding.

"We may need to reevaluate the position. The first layer needs to be higher," Calvin said into the microphone.

Mia entered notes into the tablet as the helicopter landed. This was the first time they were attempting to test the full shield. "What's next?"

"I want to put The Arabian underwater," Calvin said. "The water line may be a weakness."

They rode to the next location. The team was spread to several parts of the city. The main palace, the Sheikh's other three palaces, the main mall, Gold Souk, Spice Souk, and several highly populated areas. Calvin instructed them where to move for the next round of testing.

Calvin guided The Arabian into the Dirham River, as Mia stood at the edge of the water staring at the sky. "Is that what I think it is?" She couldn't tell what it was from that distance but knew it was deadly. Hopefully, all the mobile units were still in place.

Mia screamed, "Calvin, put up the shield now."

Chapter 26

Calvin and the team watched the news reporting that a U.S. drone missile strike was launched against a neighboring country. He remembered how the alarm in Mia's voice caused him to comply, raising the shield to protect Durabia immediately.

Thankfully, it had not been aimed at them or close enough to affect Durabia. The layer that would have protected them from a missile was still in development. The layers they did have in place worked better than he thought possible.

"What if the U.S. had dropped a bomb on Durabia?" Mia leaned closer to his ear. "What side of the fence do we stand on?"

Calvin wished he'd taken more time to make sure there was no way this technology could be abused and used against America. He was fine with global outreach, but creating protection for Americans was Calvin's first priority. Even though the government had shown they weren't to be totally trusted. He listened to a newscaster talking about a retaliatory attack on the American military base in the area as he pondered Mia's question.

"I may not agree with leadership decisions of the current administration, but I won't do anything to risk American lives."

"What would the impact of a war here have on your project?" Mia scanned the room.

"The detection system would have to become a priority." Calvin wondered if the reason for the strike was valid. He hadn't realized how complicated participating in this project would be. In everything he researched, Durabia had no history of conflict with the United States. In several wars before that time, they assisted America in every way. Calvin naively expected things to continue in the same vein well into the future. However, leadership changes—especially ones that caused so many world leaders to lose trust in America, meant nothing was certain anymore.

Mia leaned in closer to Calvin. "Can the shield be used against us in any way?"

"Only to keep us out if we end up on opposite teams." Calvin gave her hand a squeeze. His concern wasn't the shield, but The Arabians. Those hovercrafts could definitely be weaponized and used against them. He would have to reconsider their use in his contingency plan.

"Hey, we're having an emergency meeting." Daron came in and switched off the broadcast.

Khalil Germaine, Sheikh Kamran along with his nephew Hassan, and several Knights, entered the room. They all made for an impressive picture. Suits, dishdashas, and formidable expressions. Strictly business.

Khalil, the man who founded The Castle and was the main reason the Kings from America and the ruling Sheikh and his family had been brought together, stood near the monitors, holding up a hand to gain everyone's attention. "This hit a little too close to home. When Calvin arrived, he wanted to know if we planned to create one shield to protect the entire city or break it down into quadrants." He scanned everyone's faces until his dark-brown eyes landed on Calvin. "With this incident, we feel quadrants may be best until everything is up and running."

"So key places like the main palace are protected first while the large shield is put in place." Calvin agreed that breaking the shield up into quadrants was a better plan, especially since certain sites were more high risk than others. The Muslim world had it in for Sheikha Ellena. None of the palaces was a safe bet.

"Yes, how long do you think it would take to reconfigure the shield?" Khalil asked.

"At least a week for the main palace, longer for other locations you select." Calvin assumed the main palace was the number one priority.

The men rolled out of the room as quickly as they'd come in. The phone vibrated in his pocket again. Calvin glanced at the screen. "Hey, Mom."

"Are you and Mia okay?" Janine's voice was filled with concern.

"It didn't happen in the area we are in."

"They are recommending Americans leave the area as soon as possible," his dad said in the background.

"Mom, put this on speakerphone," Calvin said, and waited a second for her to comply.

"We do have plans to come back to the States, but not right now." Calvin slipped away so he was out of earshot of Mia. "Mom, I have everything handled over here. I need you to do something big for me on your end."

"What?"

"I need you to check for availability of a couple of wedding venues. I want to have all the details in hand when I approach her on setting a date." Calvin hadn't talked about the wedding recently, but it was high time to make it official. That is, if Mia was still on the same page.

"Send over the information. Be safe." Janine disconnected the line.

Daron came over to Calvin as he texted her the places. "Hey, I've arranged a night at the Diera Resort for you and Mia, under the names Mr. and Mrs. Langston."

"I appreciate that." Calvin ran a hand over his curly low afro. "We could definitely use some alone time after a day like this."

Daron patted him on the back. "Since Gabriel is still in town, there will be a protection team in the two rooms next to yours."

"Give me the number so I can arrange a couple's massage." He wanted to spoil Mia tonight and remind her how important she was to him. He hated that Daron had been the one to make all of these arrangements, but the last thing he needed was some sinister element interrupting their night.

* * *

When they entered the room, Luther Vandross crooned *If Only For One Night* and scented candles were placed throughout. The two massage tables were set up in front of glass doors leading to the balcony that perfectly displayed the sunset.

"Today was intense." Calvin slid off his jacket and tossed it on the couch. "Are you all right with winding down with a massage, then some fine food?"

Mia's smile was so bright it made his heart melt. She gave him a peck on the cheek. "I'm going to take a quick shower before they get here."

She disappeared into the bathroom. He would have loved to join her, but if he did a massage would be the last thing on his mind.

He checked to make sure everything was stocked as he'd requested with Mia's favorite drinks and appetizers. By the time he'd had his turn in the shower, there was a knock at the door. "That should be the masseurs."

Calvin let the team in. After ninety minutes of kneading away the tension of the day, the masseur left with the tables, then the food arrived. "Perfect timing."

"I miss this," Calvin said as they dined on grilled shrimp machboos, a local seafood and rice dish. "I apologize for not taking everything we had on deck when I accepted this project. If you're ready to have kids, I'll talk with Daron about having someone else take over."

"I've had a lot of time to think since I've been here. I've realized that I took Diana's death harder than I thought, and it had me rushing into everything." She put her hand over his. "Just because life is too short doesn't mean I have to squeeze all aspects of our lives in so soon. It also means that I can't procrastinate on things that are important to me."

Calvin poured more wine into their glasses. "Well, there's one thing that I hope we'll stop dragging our feet on. It's beyond time for you to officially become Mrs. Atwood."

Mia sipped her Moscato and gave him a weak smile.

"Let's address the other elephant in the relationship." Calvin hoped this wasn't the reason for her lackluster response to his comment. "How is Avant going to fit into your life?"

"No. I care for him. We were able to share our grief and memories of Diana. Since it happened during a major shift in our lives, it did blur the line for me a bit." Mia averted her gaze to the table, then took a sip from the glass. "Honestly, I have to ask. Do you ever see yourself stepping back from your work enough for us to actually start a family? Without any resentment?"

"I was watching a show online where the main character put his family in danger to run the country." He stood, gently pulling Mia to her feet before guiding her to the couch. "I felt conflicted about it. I understand the pull of purpose and responsibility, but all the maneuvering required to make it happen and the effect on his family bothered me."

She leaned into his arms. "'And you're telling me this because ....'"

"It made me grateful that I wasn't in Khalil or Kamran's position." Calvin stroked Mia's soft wavy hair. "While I feel compelled to create devices that help people, I realize that my purpose doesn't have to always require us to sacrifice our happiness. I have the power to be more selective with my 'yes'."

She faced him, those dark-brown orbs gazing into his eyes. "But that doesn't answer my question."

"Sleeping alone while you're forced to stay down the hall from me made me realize that my home is with you. I will never regret that."

Chapter 27

"Why do you look so nervous?" Calvin asked, glancing over at Mia as they rode to Kamran and Ellena's penthouse near the Durabian River.

"Not nervous." Mia pushed a strand of hair behind her ear. "I was just thinking about how Ellena's simple good deed resulted in her marrying Kamran, someone so high up on the food chain. That was … interesting. Stuff like that doesn't ever happen to me."

Calvin relaxed a bit. Mia had been unusually quiet over the past few days. Kamran and Ellena were known to entertain in their Free Zone residence to make guests more comfortable. After the drone strike, the more formal environment of the palace would not place Mia in a position to open up to Ellena. This was a chance for her to speak with the Sheikha, who might be able to allay some of her concerns. Kamran had tasked Calvin with the biggest challenge of his life. Back in the States the concept was monumental, but executing it was an entirely different beast. But he wouldn't trade this experience for the world. Mia could be more of an asset here than in America. Would she ever be able to see that?

"Well, I certainly hope our relationship rates up there," he teased about the statement of Ellena and the food chain. "I'd like to think I'm a good catch."

She gasped, slapped a playful hand to his arm. "Oh, I didn't mean—"

"I know what you meant, sweetheart," he said, giving her hand a gentle pat. "I'm amazed by their whirlwind courtship, but still surprised that his family put them in the center of a plot to make sure Kamran never sat on the Durabian throne. Boggles my mind that so many would have a problem with their union in this day and age."

"Our day. Our age. Not theirs. But if it hadn't happened, we wouldn't be here," she said. "I'm beginning to like it more and more. It's just sometimes I do miss home. I feel like I'm always overthinking things to make sure that I don't overstep or overstate here. I'm so far out of my element."

Calvin wondered if that was true or if Mia was telling him what she thought he needed to hear. "That's not it at—"

Nicco glanced at them in the rearview mirror. "We're here. Roc will escort you up to the top level."

"I'll be waiting outside when you're ready to go," Roc added as he held the door open for them.

Calvin handed her the bottle of Cabernet Sauvignon nestled in the seat between them, then grabbed the sparkling cider—a sign of respect that Kamran may not drink alcohol, while Ellena still indulged from time to time.

He took a deep breath as they rode the elevator. Calvin really hoped this would be a perfect opportunity for Mia to speak to Ellena and discuss issues that she might have as a Black woman in the Middle East. While every person's experience was different, the loneliness that Mia thought she was hiding was prevalent. He hoped Mia devoloped a sisterhood with Ellena that would help ease her transition.

The doors of the elevator opened. Calvin placed the palm of his hand on Mia's lower back and escorted her to the wide silver doors. The place was elaborately decorated in the same fashion as the palace, with shades of rich purples and golds, but also had an American cosmopolitan feel that had Ellena's touch all over.

"Welcome. Kamran is out on the balcony." Ellena gestured toward the glass door leading to a balcony that stretched the length of the living room all the way to the parlor. "You gentlemen can talk business before dinner, while Mia and I have a little woman chat."

Calvin glanced over at Mia. She nodded, taking the sparkling cider from his hand.

"We brought drinks." Mia followed Ellena toward the living room, then to the kitchen. The curvaceous woman was regal in a lavender tunic that had a small sheer train. Her eyes held a bit of sadness despite the smile. Her complexion was slightly darker than Mia's own ivory one. Sheikh Kamran couldn't seem to keep his eyes off her, and that brought a smile to Calvin's face.

"My father taught me to never show up empty-handed to dinner."

"Smart man," she said with a smile.

Calvin stepped on the balcony which looked over the entire city. The buildings seemed to glow in the dusk.

Kamran gestured to one of the seats. "Thanks for coming out this evening."

"I appreciate the invite." Calvin lowered himself into the chair.

"The drone strike confirmed that bringing you here was indeed the best decision," Kamran stated, looking out at the sunset. "Now that I know Durabia will be more secure, I plan to have my nephew pick up Ellena's niece, Blair. She is a surgical nurse with an ex-husband who's a bit of a troublemaker. I think Hassan can handle things"

Calvin put his cell on vibrate, ignoring a call from his parents. "I believe you want to know how long it will be before the shield is installed to protect the designated free zone areas."

"Yes."

"Probably not as quickly as you would like," Calvin said, filtering all of the remaining issues in his mind. "The drone strike has caused us to split the team into parts so that we're working on the shield twenty-four hours a day to reduce the time it will take to complete."

Kamran turned to face Calvin with a concerned expression etched on his face. "As you know, Ellena's experience in Nadaum will make her family a target."

Calvin was aware that Ellena had been taken and that the Kings, Knights, and Daron's Crossroads Security team went into Nadaum and also Durabia in a daring dual rescue.

"How good is she with a weapon?"

"She was trained by Alejandro Reyes."

Calvin's head whipped to him. "Seriously?"

"She had to be. It was part of her conditions of allowing her to stay here in Durabia without him or any of the Kings as part of a bodyguard detail."

"Wow," Calvin whispered. "I didn't know that part."

"Not many people do. The less people are aware of her capabilities…"

"What I can do is provide personal protection gear until we can get the shield in designated free zones."

"That will work." Kamran stood and Calvin did the same. "Let's see what the ladies are up to."

Calvin followed Kamran into the formal living room, decorated with cream furniture and purple and gold accents. They made it to the sofa just as Ellena asked Mia a question that threw him for a loop.

"Would you ever give Calvin a hall pass?" Ellena took a sip of wine as the two women lounged on the couch. The smell of fresh mint, lemon, and an array of spices wafted in the air.

Kamran's gaze locked onto his wife.

Mia flinched, then huffed, "No."

"You were quick with that response," Calvin said with a hearty chuckle.

Ellena and Mia's head snapped in their direction.

"Beloved, I see you are having an interesting conversation." Kamran leaned down to kiss Ellena on the forehead, then rested his hand lovingly on her shoulder. "Why would you ask such a thing?"

"I was just telling Mia about Mandy." Ellena placed the wine glass on the table. "My sister had a rather unique experience with a wife who actually gave her husband a conditional hall pass when their marriage was already struggling. The whole scenario left me speechless."

"I imagine it created more drama than the wife expected," Mia said, her gaze focused on Calvin, who was concerned by the tension in Mia's shoulders.

"You don't know the half of it, but we'll have to discuss that later,"

Ellena replied, glancing at her watch. "The rest of the guests are on their way up, and we'll have to tone down the conversation with the children present."

"Just one question, though," Mia said in a tone that was too calm for Calvin's liking.

Ellena shifted her gaze from Kamran to Mia who said, "How is a conditional hall pass that much different from a husband having multiple wives? Kamran is able to take on a few more, right?"

Kamran moved forward to collect his wife before she let loose with something that could not be taken back.

So much for bonding. The unease crackled in the air as both ladies stood. Calvin took Mia's hand and said a silent prayer that this night didn't do more harm than good with Mia's mindset about being in Durabia.

Kamran led them to a dining room that seated at least eighteen people, but kept his gaze on Ellena as she struggled to keep her composure. "We should have had a dinner welcoming you to the family and Durabia when you first arrived. But tonight, we will correct that."

As the remainder of guests arrived with their children, Calvin was introduced to Mandy and Chaz along with Kamran's nephew Hassan. Calvin had encountered Hassan at a Castle meeting, but hadn't had an opportunity to know him on a more personal level. The dinner conversation was light as they enjoyed a salad made from tomatoes, green onions and cucumber, basmati rice and seasoned chicken, smoked eggplant, beef and lamb kabob, and several other dishes. The children were taken into a back room as the adults scattered between the dining room and living room.

Kamran left Mandy and Chaz, and led Ellena across the room to Mia and Calvin.

"Ellena has concerns about certain family members who remain on palace grounds." Kamran wrapped an arm lovingly around her waist.

"What do you want to happen?" Calvin asked.

Ellena took a sip of wine then answered, "I want the royal prisoners moved from the palace and to be alerted if they make an unauthorized attempt to return."

Calvin glanced over at Mia who kept a neutral expression on her face. "Daron and I can work on something." They'd already modified the tracking tattoo technology to alert Daron's team when anyone went outside the allotted boundary.

Rahm, one of the Knights of the Castle, immediately popped in his mind. He was scheduled to come to Durabia soon, and could put tattoos on the prisoners. Rahm had been given a second chance at life after paying for a crime he didn't commit. Calvin wondered if his girlfriend, Marilyn, was having a problem with the move overseas like Mia. From clips of conversation he'd overheard, Rahm's family drama and someone from his past wanting revenge was complicating things. He'd talk it over with Daron because at this point, it was the only feasible idea.

Kamran smiled. "I am looking forward to hearing what you come up with."

"Mia, I wanted to apologize for earlier." Ellena gave an awkward half smile. "Having multiple wives is a sensitive topic."

Mia smiled in return. "I wasn't trying to be judgmental, I was just thinking about the different angles of the hall pass question. When women take a cheating man back that's an unofficial hall pass. Either way, Mandy definitely benefited well from someone's decision to give one."

Calvin nudged Mia in the side to silence her.

Ellena glanced at a man speaking with Hassan who had the same olive complexion, dark hair and features of both the Khan and Maharaj families. "He is handsome, isn't he? Seems there's no shortage of handsome men in this family."

Kamran drew Ellena's body closer to his as Mandy and Chaz walked toward them. "Beloved, behave."

Calvin grinned. He appreciated Kamran's strategy of making sure he was connected to who he was protecting. This unconventional family was each doing their part to transform Durabia.

Chapter 28

Mia was surprised when she received an early morning call and found out that Avant was in Durabia on business. A tinge of guilt pinched her heart, because she was excited to be with someone not associated with Calvin and the project. A nice way to end her day off. Mia's conversation with Ellena about hall passes, cheating, and multiple wives flashed in her mind for a moment, as she noticed how his light gray shirt hugged his muscles.

"Hey beautiful." Avant smiled when he saw her standing near the bar.

Mia stepped back when Avant went to hug her. "You're looking good."

While she'd seen people do it without retribution, she had also heard a story of a woman arrested and placed in jail for greeting a male friend with a kiss on the cheek.

She probably would get an ear full later for ditching her security guards.

"Toya asked about you." Avant waved over the bartender.

Mia scanned the drink menu. "How is she?"

"Good. Ready for her next adventure." Avant ordered Jack and Coke. "Her mom may be in over her head. Her blackmail story keeps changing. Do you know of a company in her area that can discreetly investigate what's going on?"

"I'll find you someone. I'll also review the information you gave Daron then cross check some things." She paused, ordering an apple martini. "Hopefully, it's nothing."

"Hopefully."

Mia knew there was a lot he wasn't saying, but she didn't push. They were in a public setting, and maybe he didn't want to say too much. "When do you have to be back in the States?"

"Two days, and then I have to find out what my cousin has really gotten herself into." Avant rested his elbow on the countertop, angling his body toward her. "She's more like a sister than a cousin. Recently, she apologized to me, but what she was actually saying didn't make sense. Had me plenty worried and gave me chills."

Mia couldn't help noticing a group of men sitting nearby, watching them intently. Evidently, Avant's cousin wasn't the only one in trouble. "Have you had any more weird random conversations lately?"

The bartender placed their drinks in front of them as Avant's handsome face crumpled into a frown. "No, why?"

"Just wondering." Mia sipped the martini, letting the green liquid slide down her throat. Her focus was on the men lounging in the rear area of the place, not drinking or talking. One glanced down at his phone then looked up at Avant. The burly guy next to him simply nodded then stood, walking to the end of the bar to their left. "Do you have any more meetings before you leave?"

Avant retrieved his phone and scrolled through the calendar app. "One tomorrow."

Leaning closer but making sure not to touch, she whispered, "I believe you were targeted for your excellent ability to recall information."

"How would that be beneficial to anyone?" Avant sipped his drink and glanced cautiously around the bar, pausing momentarily on the burly guy.

"I'm not sure." Mia glanced at her phone, checking for messages that might mention if the team had been aware of the men in the bar. "Let's walk to the elevator. We'll just have to enjoy a private conversation in your room."

Avant waved the bartender over and took care of the bill.

She watched a total of seven men spread out over the room and followed them. "See if you can change your flight and leave early."

Avant's gaze narrowed as the men moved in their direction.

"Once you're in your room, don't open the door for anyone. Don't order room service. I'll get you a security detail for your meeting tomorrow." Mia pressed the elevator button hoping it would come before the men reached them.

Avant scanned the area. "Okay."

The doors opened and Mia rushed them in quickly, pressing the close button repeatedly. The men sprinted forward, and one managed to get his hand in the door. Four men stepped in.

Mia immediately activated her tracking earring.

"Mr. Arrington," the tallest guy said as he turned to Avant, pointing a gun at his chest. "Your plans for the evening have changed. You'll both be coming with us."

Avant glanced over at Mia, giving her an unspoken apology.

Mia allowed herself to be taken, because odds weren't in her favor. Her knives against their guns. She had to wait for a better opportunity to make a move. They were led into a bedroom suite and tied up with zip ties.

"I'm so sorry, Mia," Avant whispered once they were left alone in the room.

"Help is on the way." Mia listened to see if she could hear the men on the other side of the door. "We just have to make sure we don't get separated or do anything to get ourselves killed. Understood?"

"No one knows we've been taken." Avant struggled trying to break free.

"My people know, but they'll need time to put a plan in place." Mia lifted her shirt slightly, twisting to reach the knife clipped on her waistband.

Mia scanned the room for plausible weapons, all the while making a personal vow. If she survived this, she'd enjoy being with Calvin first and foremost—everything was secondary. After that she'd decide if she wanted to remain in this line of work or start a family.

"What are you thinking about?" Avant asked.

"My future." Mia sliced through her bonds and went over to free him. "Everything in me is screaming it's time to move. I'm going to trust my instinct."

Mia crept to the door, opening it ever so slightly to eye the guard standing just outside. She held a palm up to Avant to halt his movements. Scanning the room for a weapon, she picked up a lamp. Opening the door suddenly, she smashed the man over the head. As he crumpled to the floor, she cut the cord off the lamp and tied up the guard, grabbed his gun, and moved into the other room.

"What now?" Avant cautiously followed into the living room.

"We need to find out if the rest of the crew is blocking our exit." She couldn't believe they'd only left one person guarding the door. But they were tied up, so maybe they didn't consider them a threat.

Shifting the tiny metal on the peephole on the door, she peered through the round glass looking into the hallway. No one was in her line of sight.

"When I open this door, we need to run for the stairs. Then we'll catch the elevator on the next level," Mia instructed.

"Okay."

Mia swung the door open. She didn't make it out two feet before two men appeared to her right. One grabbed her arm. She punched him hard, as Avant's fist connected with the other guy's jaw.

They raced for the stairs. The elevator opened and four of the men from earlier stepped out in front of them. They changed direction and headed toward the other end of the corridor.

"How did they get out?" the tallest of the group asked.

"Damn, they couldn't have come five minutes later," Mia said, firing several shots before hustling down the corridor.

Just as they reached the room where they escaped, the door across the hall from it opened.

Several armed men stepped out, stopping them in their tracks. Mia looked back. Nowhere to go.

"Drop the gun."

Mia reluctantly let the weapon fall to the carpeted floor. They ushered them back into the suite. This time, their hands were handcuffed behind their backs. Not much of a concern because Mia knew how to get out of the cuffs. The escape had failed, but it did result in gaining some insight. Now she knew the best way out. Mia just needed another opening to make a second attempt.

Several minutes later, four men entered. They sat Avant at a desk and Mia in a chair in the corner of the room. Mia cringed as she recognized the blonde man who walked over and lowered himself into the chair next to Avant.

"Mr. Arrington, it's a pleasure to make your acquaintance." He placed a laptop in front of Avant. "We have work to do."

"I'm not sure how I can help." Avant glanced at the laptop, then the man standing closest to him.

"I need you to do what you do. Analyze the data and tell me which will be most profitable in the long run."

Avant opened the lid of the personal computer. "If you send the data to Saber's Financial system, I can provide that information to you within four hours."

"You'll have to work with what's on the laptop." He pulled out his Sig Sauer, a nine-millimeter pistol. "Unless you want to die now. Your flight leaves in two days. Do you want to be in a passenger seat or underneath in a coffin?"

Avant opened the laptop. "What's the login?"

"The answer for number twenty-one in Toya's workbook."

Avant cut his eyes back at Mia. His fingers typed tentatively at first.

Gabriel stood and turned, finally noticing Mia. "What do we have here?"

"Sorry, we had to take her too," the stockier guy standing next to Mia said.

"My bonus prize." Gabriel gave an evil snarl, moving toward Mia. "What to do with you? Seeing that you're here with another man may mean that things aren't so good with you and Calvin Atwood, eh? This could certainly work in my favor."

She was pretty sure Gabriel had not figured out how to make Calvin's protection pod work properly. "Why are you wasting Avant's time running a profitability analysis on a product you don't have finished yet?" Mia now understood that they were trying to reduce the digital footprint that would trace back to Gabriel. She also suspected that this wouldn't be a one-time deal with Avant.

"I have a feeling you may be the solution to that problem." Gabriel lifted her roughly by the arm from the plush chair and attempted to cuff her to a wooden chair. The design wouldn't allow for it. "Get the other pair."

"Whatever you're thinking will never work," Mia stated as a man came back with what looked like prison transport cuffs.

This time the guard lifted her up while Gabriel attached the nylon band with the D ring to the chair. He shoved her back down, cuffing her hands behind. "Hopefully, Atwood loves you more than you love him."

Chapter 29

Calvin stared at the vacant chair next to him. He appreciated Daron setting up a station for Mia within the lab. He had only mentioned it to him in passing that he hated Mia standing outside his work area most of the day. He should take a page out of Daron's book. Listening to the things Mia said that seemed small, but were actually really important, and making them a reality. Calvin wanted to show Mia he cared and was paying attention to her in both small and big ways.

"Are you gonna be all right without Mia here today?" Roc teased.

"Yeah. Yeah." He waved the smiling man off, then focused his attention on the screen. "I'm curious why Daron has a smaller team today?"

"He's hoping that it'll make it harder for them to figure out your actual location by splitting up the team between several of the testing areas."

"They're looking for me?" Calvin knew Gabriel was in the area, but hadn't realized he was actively trying to get the protection pod. "Is Mia ..."

"Mia is aware of the situation," Roc assured. "If she sees any sign of trouble, she'll reach out to us."

Calvin grabbed the controller and attached it to his forearm. "Well we shouldn't draw too much attention today. We're just setting up some checks and balances in the main system for the remote launches."

The remote launch was if the Kings deemed it necessary to put up the shield without making a call to the detection team. However, they wanted to make sure no one could get the remote, activate the shield, then release a toxin. Today was about going through several different protocols to figure out the best one. All the brainstorming sessions on how this protective shield could be used against them was disheartening, but it was the reality. Whatever he created, someone was working just as hard to figure out how to bypass it or use it for some evil purpose.

"I'll let you and the team get to it." Roc went to his position outside the glass door.

Calvin hadn't realized how fast the day had gone by until an alarm went off. He checked, it wasn't the shield. The chair clattered to the ground as Calvin sprang to his feet. Mia was in trouble. Her earring tracker had been activated.

"Hey, have Nicco bring the truck around." He rushed through the lab toward Roc. Pulling out his cell, he called Daron while following Roc to the SUV.

"I'm heading to Mia's location."

"I've got a local team that will meet you there," Daron assured him. "Please let them handle it. We do not want you in the middle of an incident. We're not at home and have to tread carefully."

"Understood," Calvin lied. He would die if it meant saving Mia. He would do whatever was needed to make sure she was safe. At the moment, until they were in place to extract her from whatever harm had come her way, he said a prayer for her safety.

Roc held the door open and he slid into the back.

What if … Calvin was kicking himself for having this long of an engagement. They should have been married. Now she was in trouble, and he was too far away to be of any help.

"Are you still there?" Daron asked.

Calvin watched as one SUV headed out first. "Yes."

Mia activating her earrings forced Calvin to accept that he'd played a big part in messing up his ideal life. He hadn't noticed the change in the way Mia had responded to the delay in confirming a wedding date. He still felt like they had time, but losing a friend had made her feel like she didn't have time to waste. Now he was feeling the same way.

"Cameron has landed. If you need her, call her," Daron advised him. "I'm arranging a flight out of Nadaum now."

"I'll call her. Maybe she can get there faster than I can." His leg bounced up and down with nervous energy as they exited the secured area and hit the main road.

"The fact that she is in the city and appears to be in a hotel is a good sign," Daron explained. "I have someone working to see if they can get access to the security cameras. When I do, I'll send it to the team."

"Are you buckled up?" Nicco called out. "It looks like we may have a situation."

"What's going on?" Daron asked.

Calvin strapped in. "A truck is gaining on the lead SUV."

"Turn on your suit now. Make sure the heat shield is on," Daron urged Calvin.

Roc glanced back over his shoulder. "Hold on."

Calvin held onto the passenger seat in front of him. He glanced over as the sound of gunfire erupted and bullets pinged off the lead SUV.

"Why today?" Calvin asked peering out of the rear window in time to see a vehicle coming at them at a high rate of speed. The truck shifted hard enough to jerk him around the seat.

"Did you hear me?" Daron asked. "Hang up and turn on your cloaking!"

Calvin slid the phone in his pocket. The idea of not reaching Mia in time popped into his head as his body jerked forward at the impact of being rear ended.

"Shit," Roc muttered.

He was reaching toward his wrist to activate the Emperor's Suit when another big boom and the sound of metal crushing filled the air. Another vehicle slammed them from the side, causing the SUV to roll on its side and slide a few feet before coming to a complete stop. Calvin was pressed against the door as Roc and Nicco were tossed about.

This can't be happening. Now he had to survive his own situation to get to Mia.

Chapter 30

Calvin's body throbbed to a beat the pain had etched out, but at least he was alive. The controller for the Arabian had tightened around his arm, but the unit hadn't been damaged. He'd need to cut it off later, but that was the least of his worries. Gunfire blasted in the distance.

"The team up ahead is holding off a group heading our way. We need to move," Nicco groaned.

"All we want is Calvin Atwood," a gruff voice called out from beyond the vehicle.

"Turn on your suit," Roc said, pulling out a gun and sliding on the glasses that allowed him to see Calvin with the device on.

Calvin complied, saying, "They already know I'm in here."

"Not for much longer," Roc said as one of the men tried to break into the bulletproof window.

"Climb into the trunk." Roc unbuckled his seatbelt and nodded for Nicco to move to the back seat. He shifted to the driver's seat with his back against the door and his gun pointing up toward the passenger window.

Calvin crawled over the seat into the trunk of the Range Rover. Needles of pain pricked every move. Nicco followed him, shifting the black crate in the back. "How many of them are there?"

"Three that I can see," Nicco answered.

Roc climbed over the seats to the back. He peered out of the rear as the banging on the passenger window stopped.

"What's the plan?" Calvin asked.

"Open the trunk, then head up there." Roc pointed to a sandy dune a few hundred yards away. Bullets rained down on the passenger window. Eventually they'd penetrate the glass.

"And you?" Calvin hated that Roc and Nicco weren't coming with him.

"I'm going to buy you some time." Roc unholstered his weapon. "You've gotta move fast once the trunk opens."

Nicco grabbed one of the larger guns that had been stored in the back. "Watch your footprints."

The glass shattered, crashing in. A man peered into the SUV. "They're escaping out the back."

Calvin nodded as Roc lifted the trunk. He quietly slipped out. Boots pounded the pavement toward them and gunfire filled the air. Calvin paused, wishing he'd grabbed one of the smaller guns out of the crate in the trunk.

Nicco fired off several shots that sent the men diving for cover. One man fell at the fender of the truck behind them. In the distance, the lead SUV traded shots with another vehicle.

Calvin ducked behind the vehicle that hit them instead of going up the dune. He yanked on the handle. "Damn it!" *Who locks a door in a situation like this?*

Six other men rushed Nicco and Roc, surrounding them. Their weapons clattered to the ground.

Roc stood in front of the gun men. "Where is he?"

"I don't know." Roc and Nicco were lined up against the Range Rover.

"Then you die first." Calvin sprinted toward one of the discarded guns. Maybe he could get a shot off and give Daron's team a chance.

Before he made it to the weapon, the man fired.

Roc was suddenly covered in a protection pod, and a wall protection device appeared in front of Nicco. All six gunmen hit the ground. Only one man was moving, wrestling for the gun with what seemed like an invisible man. Daron couldn't have possibly arrived in time. The man finally stopped stirring, and Cameron materialized among the bodies. He had no idea where she'd come from.

"Grab the gear out of the back. Your new ride is back there." Cameron pointed to the vehicle behind him. She slung the strap of the assault rifle over her head. "Get Calvin out of here."

"What about Mia?" Calvin asked as Roc slipped out of the protection pod and rushed in the direction of the Range Rover.

"You and the team are heading her way. That's why they need the gear." Cameron grabbed the discarded protection pod and wall shield.

They grabbed the crate from the back and maneuvered to the vehicle Cameron pointed out. "Are you coming?"

"I should be minutes behind you." Cameron peered into the Range Rover. "Make sure everyone has communication devices, including Calvin."

Calvin passed the first vehicle. Seven men were stretched out on the ground. The situation was bigger than he realized.

As he slid into the back seat, Roc handed him back an earpiece. On the drive to the hotel, Calvin found out that two of the four locations with Daron's teams had been hit. His heart broke when he realized the team dispatched to help Mia was one of those teams.

Chapter 31

Roc burst into the room with Calvin on his heels. Gabriel and Avant sat a desk against the wall. Gabriel's head snapped toward the door as he whipped out his Sig Sauer and pointed it at Mia.

"Amazing, how did you know she was in trouble?" Gabriel moved closer to Mia who was handcuffed to a chair.

Calvin halted his approach. "You don't want to do this."

"If you hadn't interrupted, she may have been released in a couple of hours." Gabriel aimed the weapon at Mia's head. She didn't flinch. Her gaze locked on Calvin.

"You and I both know that's a lie." Calvin watched as Roc eased toward Avant. Nicco crept along the opposite side of the wall.

Gabriel muttered something Calvin couldn't make out.

"Calvin, move," Mia yelled seconds before the door was sprayed with bullets. The door sprang open. Bullets hit the glass window and shattered it in several directions

Gabriel swung his gun towards Calvin, but Mia yanked her arm forward and swung the chair at Gabriel who stumbled towards the window. She swung a second time. Gabriel ducked, causing the chair to crash into the damaged glass.

Calvin slammed a fist into the first guy that came through the door as Gabriel tackled Mia. Roc grabbed Avant, pulling him out of the line of fire. Mia kicked Gabriel in the gut sending his back against the table. One of the shooters turned the gun on Calvin, but Nicco took him out before he could pull the trigger.

Calvin grabbed the floor lamp and bashed it over the second man's arm until his weapon hit the floor. He silently kicked himself for not already having his gun out. Calvin was clearly out of his element.

His attention immediately returned to Mia, who exchanged multiple punches with Gabriel. Nicco ran toward Mia but was hit by a stocky guy coming out of the bathroom. Gabriel grabbed Mia and threw her against the window which caved on impact.

"I hope she can fly," Gabriel sneered, pinning a gaze on Calvin.

Calvin's heart dropped at the sight of Gabriel tossing Mia out of the window.

"Shit," Cameron yelled, rushing through the door.

Calvin raced across the room, lifting his shirt sleeve and tapping the controls on his wrist device.

"What are you doing?" Roc called out.

"Don't even think about it," Cameron said.

Gabriel fell back against the window as Calvin leapt through the opening after Mia.

The hotel was near the storage center for The Arabian that protected this quadrant. From the test launch, Calvin knew how long it would take to reach the seventieth floor. *This has to work.* Calvin forced himself to concentrate on getting to Mia. He aimed his body toward her, streamlining on the descent. She was falling faster than he anticipated. Damn it! He wasn't going to reach her in time.

The concrete driveway was getting closer far too quickly. The Arabian made it into position just in time to release the protective shield material.

"Calvin, you need to spiral The Arabian the moment your body hits the material," Cameron said in his earpiece. "If you don't, you'll *both* hit that pavement—hard. That material's not easy to hold onto."

Seconds later, Mia's body slammed against the spread material. It dipped under her weight. When he joined her moments later, he tried to hold on. He couldn't grasp the flexible plastic material. He sent The Arabian spinning, and their bodies quickly became entangled. The Arabian stabilized, but Calvin couldn't see to safely land the hovercraft.

"I'm overriding the controls. I'll guide it from here," Daron announced.

Calvin grabbed Mia to his body. "Are you okay?"

She moaned, rubbing her shoulder. "I didn't go splat on the pavement, but my body may have hit that Arabian one too many times."

"How securely are you and Mia wrapped up?" Daron asked.

Calvin could barely see Mia or The Arabian, but she was breathing and managed to make a joke as well. "We're tangled pretty good."

"I'm lifting you back up then."

He was relieved when The Arabian shifted upward, back in the direction of that open window. It halted for a moment, and the rustling of the material echoed around them. Cameron and Daron extended their hands to help them out once they reached a point that was level to the carpet.

"I have never loved you and these inventions of yours more than I do right now," Mia said.

Calvin pulled Mia to his chest, rocking her in his arms. "I'm just glad it worked. While we haven't declared it officially." He planted a kiss on her forehead. "I'm committed to the 'until death to do us part' thing. But I'd love if it didn't happen for a long time."

"I can get with that plan," Mia choked up, right before crumpling into his arms.

Chapter 32

Calvin glanced at Mia's pale face as she lay stretched out on the hospital bed. Hours had passed, and he was still emotionally drained after saving Mia from falling to her death. Only to have her nearly die in his arms. He held Mia's hand and stared at the blood-soaked clothing bunched on the chair. She'd lost so much that she needed a transfusion upon arriving. Calvin rested his head on the bed. Mia had been tossing and turning and had only barely opened her eyes for the last few hours.

"I hope you buried Gabriel in some desert shit hole somewhere," Mia whispered.

Calvin's head shot up, he leaned forward to kiss her on the forehead. "I have never been so terrified in my life."

Mia shifted to a seated position in the bed. "What happened?"

He blinked several times as his chest tightened at the memory of that entire experience, and the thought of losing her had pierced a hole in his soul. "You were sliced by a piece of glass when you went through the window. You lost a lot of blood, I didn't see it at first and didn't realize how bad it was until we were pulled back into the room." Calvin slid onto the bed and wrapped his arms around her, pulling her into his chest.

"Out of everything, a piece of glass is what takes me out." Mia gave a dry cough as she glanced to her left. "What's with the drapery?"

"We're in the main palace. Daron thought it was best for our privacy." Calvin glanced in the direction of the door. "One of his people is outside at all times and notifies me before anyone enters."

"If that's what it took to be able to wake up to you by my side, I appreciate it." Mia accepted the cup of water Calvin handed her, taking a sip out of the straw. "How are you?"

"Grateful. So very, very grateful."

They stayed that way, his head pressed near the warmth of her cheek for what seemed an eternity.

"How's Avant?" she whispered.

"Probably in shock, but not injured." Calvin returned the cup to the tray and gently stroked her hair. "He wanted to stay and make sure you were okay, but Daron thought it was best for everyone that he went back to the States as scheduled."

"So he's still in Durabia." Mia shifted slightly, angling to stare into his eyes.

Calvin checked his watch. "He's probably at the airport. You've been in and out of it for hours."

"Did Daron give him an escort?" Mia asked, guilt lacing her voice.

"I understand he's important to you. We did everything to ensure his safe return." He kissed her forehead. The last thing he wanted was her worrying about Avant. "I want to apologize for allowing my ego to set us up for failure."

Mia moved the IV line before sliding her hand along his stomach. "What are you talking about?"

"I was so focused on what I do and making an impact on the world, that I only made us a priority in words and not actions." He gently stroked her hair. "I would like us to pick a date to get married."

She cuddled in his chest and sighed. "We'll figure that out once I'm released."

"After I get the phase one shield up, we're going back to the States and getting married. Bottom line."

Hearing three knocks on the door, Calvin slid from underneath Mia and back in the chair.

"Nursing staff," Roc announced.

"I didn't know you could move that fast." Mia snickered as a petite brunette entered the room.

"I do what's necessary." Calvin chuckled as she rested her head on the pillow and closed her eyes briefly.

The nurse took Mia's vitals and disconnected her IV line, then left as quietly as she had come in.

"You never did answer me on what happened to Gabriel." Mia pulled the sheet back up to her neck.

"My focus was your recovery, so I don't have a lot of information." He grabbed his phone, handing it to her. "Last update from Daron was he was in the custody of the Durabian police."

"That's much too nice for someone like him," she said in a sour tone. "Durabian prison is even better than Club Fed back home."

Chapter 33

Despite over four weeks passing since Gabriel's arrest, Calvin still needed reassurance that he was where they said he was. He settled in the space next to Daron, waiting for the security feed to materialize on the tablet. Soon Gabriel appeared, dripping sweat, in what seemed to be a filthy prison cell.

"That's not a Durabian prison," Calvin said, peering at the screen and taking in the unfamiliar surroundings.

"Right," Daron said. "I think Mia would be pleased by his new accommodations. We can't allow you to physically see him, because he's catching all the heat for the hotel incident," Daron explained cutting the feed.

"I understand." Calvin's movements had been restricted to his new home in the Free Zone near the palace, and the palace itself. "But I need to know that the bastard won't use the American government to wiggle his way out of this."

"Because of the damage done to the hotel, we had to let Durabian police handle it." Daron placed the tablet in a duffle bag. "Trust and believe we already have a plan in place if Gabriel manages to get released or simply deported. Sheikha Ellena was especially concerned that he be held in a place that befitted the crime."

Calvin gave a low throaty chuckle. "I knew I liked that woman. Did you confirm whether or not he was involved in my attack?" Calvin went to the window to peer out at Mia's place, which wouldn't be necessary in coming weeks. After his heart to heart with Daron, he had clarity on how to make these next three years in the Middle East great for him and his soon to be wife. Things were changing under Sheikh Kamran's rule. The experiences that Mia feared most were not as much of an issue any longer.

Daron nodded. "You and Avant were scheduled to be taken to Nadaum around midnight that night. They still want you, so we will have to remain diligent about your safety." Daron wound his way towards the living room, preparing to leave. "After today, anytime you head out to work on the project you'll have to be in the Emperor's Suit in cloaking mode."

"I'll do whatever is necessary. We can't have a repeat of what happened." Calvin picked up his notebook. The team had finished building enough of the first layer of the shield to protect the palace.

He was surprised when he stepped out to see Mia and nine SUVs waiting outside for the short ride. After the incident, he had a better appreciation for the large convoy.

"You're ready for this." Daron motioned to the Kings and Knights who slipped into the vehicles and held the door open to the vehicle stationed behind the lead car.

"As long as you are, I am." Calvin slid into the back with Mia.

Today, they were testing the phase one shield around the palace and doing a temporary install if it worked.

"The Kings and Knights will surround the palace and make sure no one interrupts," Daron explained as they made their way down the secured strip of road leading to that stretch of building that covered almost five American city blocks in each direction.

Mia glanced at Calvin's notes. "We're testing the second shield design?"

"Yes. We still have to work out some safety features so nobody gets hurt when it goes up." Calvin jotted down a few elements he wanted in the final design.

"And also prevent the shield from getting damaged," Daron added, knowing they were still debating how to make the shield appear to be a part of the natural landscape. "Today the Knights and the Kings are our safety feature."

The Range Rover pulled over to the side as they neared the palace security checkpoint. The red and white barrier arm lifted, allowing a couple of the SUVs through. The remaining vehicles took the road leading to the other entry points. The only area of the grounds without a protection wall was the beach area near the gulf. Calvin stepped out of the vehicle, aiming to make it to the unit near the guard checkpoint.

"I wanted the liquid to work, but we'd have to have additional security on the tanks to make sure they're not tampered with. Then there was high risk of The Arabians with the second layer not attaching properly, which made bringing the shield down a challenge." Calvin checked the measurements and the distance before instructing the team to shift the unit back.

"How does it work?" Mia asked as they walked to the next unit.

"The layer is still similar to a gas mask." Calvin pulled out an octagon shaped piece of translucent plastic from his gear bag and placed it in her hands. "It opens like the wall shield, but they lock into each other once they touch."

"The challenge was building it to open at the same rate and speed as the liquid formula released into the air," Daron added.

Mia handed the piece back to him, then ran a hand over the unit that looked like a decorative design.

"The liquid shield would still be used in an emergency, if the entire city needed coverage, until we complete phase one." Calvin signaled Daron he was ready for the testing to commence.

"Everybody clear the testing zone," Daron called out, then counted down from five and released the device.

Seeing the shield expand and link the units together across the ground as it grew in height filled Calvin with pride. He timed how long it took to complete the entire dome. They all took a few more steps back as the helicopter passed over dropping water on the shield.

Testing with different toxic agents would continue in the lab until he was satisfied it would hold under anything imaginable.

"We can mark this testing a success," Calvin said after receiving confirmation no liquid had permeated into the palace area.

Daron glanced at Mia, then leaned into Calvin whispering, "Cameron has taken care of that other situation for you."

Chapter 34

Mia was excited to be back in the States, even if for only two weeks. She was even more thrilled to be spending time—just her and Calvin, no work, simply reconnecting. Right after they touched down in Chicago, they had made the trip to city hall with her dad and his parents and gotten married without a fuss that day. Neither of them had felt like wasting any more time after their experience in Durabia. They were supposed to be heading for dinner with the parents in Naperville.

"Why are we in Downers Grove?" Mia asked, glancing as they passed the office building that held one of the wedding venues she had originally picked.

Calvin smiled as he pulled into the driveway near the hotel. "Sticking with the plan."

Mia looked at Cameron who stood right outside the main revolving door. "You didn't?"

"I switched up a few things, but I don't think you'll be too mad at me." He leaned over, kissing her. "I didn't want you to be cheated out of a real wedding,"

"We'll see." Mia smiled, then embraced him.

Cameron rapped her knuckles against the window.

"See you in an hour," Calvin said, unlocking the door.

"Are you ready for a whirlwind makeover?" Cameron asked as Mia stepped out of the car.

"I guess so." Mia hadn't been excited about an actual wedding while recovering from Diana's death, but was now sure that she was ready to share this moment with her friends and family. "I can't wait to see what I'm wearing."

"I hope you don't mind that I commandeered the role of maid of honor," Cameron explained as she led her to the elevator. "Or that your bridal party is extremely small."

"Not at all," Mia replied, sliding in before the silver doors closed. "Who picked my wedding gown?"

"You'll know once you see it," Cameron said as they stepped off the elevator and walked down the hall to the room.

The moment she stepped into the suite and laid eyes on the white, silver and peach sequined dress hanging on the outside of the closet door, she knew. The tears couldn't be contained. "Diana," she whispered.

Mia had never been happier that she had shown Cameron a picture of the dress Diana picked out, hoping to get her opinion.

"I figured you'd be fine with the non-traditional option if it meant having a little bit of Diana with you today." Cameron knocked on the walnut door.

"You were right." Mia hugged Cameron as the makeup artist and hairstylist filtered into the parlor.

"Okay, let's get those tears wiped up and make some magic happen," Cameron said, handing Mia a silk tote bag and pointing her in the direction of the bathroom.

After changing into the under garments needed for the dress, a woman with a small afro began the process of pulling her hair into a classic love knot, while a petite brunette showered her with a light application of cosmetics.

Now that she was slipping into the dress, Mia could see the gown had been altered to have a train that made her feel more like a queen than a bride. She stepped into her white and silver heels feeling like a Queen. A photographer came and took a couple of pictures.

"All right it's time to head over." Cameron ushered everyone out of the suite, handing Mia a white coat.

Mia was nervous on the short ride to the office building, as if she wasn't already married to the man.

"Are you okay?" Cameron asked, helping Mia out of the van.

"Yes, I'm eager to see what the room looks like." Mia entered the office building just behind her meddlesome Aunt Sonya, who was notorious for being late.

"Is she really having her wedding in a corporate office space?" Sonya asked her husband as they walked through the turnstile toward the event space. The disdain in her voice wasn't hard to miss.

"As long as she's happy, that's all that matters." He placed his hand on the small of her back as they headed down the stairs.

"Oh, it's beautiful," her aunt exclaimed as she made it close to the bottom stairs.

Mia took in the lake and the splendor of orange, red and yellow leaves on the trees in the forest preserve through the wall of glass in the reception area, which provided its own brand of beauty. The highboy tables, covered with winter white cloth, held candles contained in tall glass vases.

When she touched down on the bottom of the stairs, her father was waiting. Cameron took her coat and undid the bustling of her train.

"You look gorgeous." Mason pulled her into his massive arms. "You're only missing one thing."

"What's that?" Mia frowned.

Mason produced a diamond bracelet from his jacket pocket. "It was your mother's."

Mia held out her wrist as the piano played a soft and beautiful melody.

"Your something old." He clasped the jewelry onto her wrist. "Her mom gave it to her on our wedding day."

"Dad, you're going to make me cry." Mia smiled, tracing the diamonds with the tips of her fingers.

"Just wanted to give you something special that I know she'd want you to have."

Mia squeezed him tightly.

"Sorry to break up this father-daughter moment, but I'm about to go through the door which means you and Mia are up next as soon as the song changes." Cameron handed Mia her bouquet of peach roses, then moved her closer to the door and adjusted her train.

"I guess I'll know where I'm going when I enter." Mia hooked her arm through her dad's as Cameron stepped into the room.

"That's what I'm here for," Mason said as the music changed to So Amazing by Luther Vandross.

Mia glided through the aisle of tables, her eyes lingering on the peach and silver sparkly centerpieces gracing the white tables.

The moment she looked up and saw Cameron standing in peach and Daron in the gray suit with peach tie, she held on a little tighter to her dad's arm. Calvin had never looked more handsome wearing a dashing white tux with a silver tie with a peach boutonniere.

Khalil said a prayer over their union and then in his humorous and spirit-filled fashion, gave them tidbits of wisdom, before giving them space to speak their vows. Truly from the heart, since they weren't rehearsed.

"I belong to you mind, body, and soul. We are meant to be. Being with you feels like home, it just feels right." She slid her hands into his and he held on tight. "You're my friend, lover, husband and future father to my children. Loving you is second nature, like breathing. My destiny is woven into you. My forever is with you. I let my heart take a chance just to be loved by you and it's one of the best decisions I have made."

A few murmurs of assent and heartfelt "awwws" echoed from the well-wishers.

"You, Mia Jakob, now Atwood, enhance my life in ways that I never imagined. We're better together because we challenge, nurture, and inspire each other in a way that elevates, empowers and enriches us. There is no one else I'd want to go through the ups and down of life with. I love you with everything I am."

Everyone applauded and cheered them, and took a few moments to settle down.

Bruce handed Janine a tissue. She squeezed her husband's hand as she beamed at Calvin and Mia.

"Is that everything?" Khalil asked, raising a brow.

Calvin smiled. "Yes, I think that's it."

"None of that until death do us part?" he teased

"Been there," Calvin said.

Mia nodded. "Done that."

Khalil chuckled and so did everyone else. "On that note, I now pronounce you husband and wife. Everyone, I present to you Mr. and Mrs. Calvin and Mia Atwood, the Knight and the Lady of South Holland."

A roar went up among the Kings and the rest of the Knights who were stationed around the room, as the onlookers shared curious glances before realizing this was also something to celebrate. Khalil handed Calvin a Castle pendant and then a diamond Castle bracelet for Mia.

"Hey, what about the kiss the bride part?" Calvin protested.

"Didn't I see you stealing one before the wedding?" Khalil said, grinning. "That counts. But just in case ..." He gestured for them to have at it.

Calvin brought Mia to his side. Cameron quickly bustled Mia's train before following Daron to the table with the Atwoods and Mason. Mia looked at Calvin confused.

"We're about to have our first dance as husband and wife," Calvin answered her unasked question.

"A little backwards, isn't it?"

"Nothing about our marriage is going to be normal."

The wait staff wound their way through the banquet tables serving soup and salad, as their song, Adorn by Miguel, played after a signal from Daron.

Mia wrapped her arms around his neck. "I can't believe you pulled this off."

"I hope you didn't mind me throwing the wedding in between the reception and dinner," Calvin said, as their bodies swayed to the rhythm.

"It's perfect, despite the reception taking place while I was getting dressed." Mia was surprised to see Avant there. However, she did notice that Calvin had seated him with several of her single friends far away from her table. *Well played, Calvin. Well played.*

"You stole my breath when you entered the room. I thought I might have to call in an Arabian to help me stand."

"You're silly," Mia said as Calvin began moving her across the dance floor, showing off his stepping moves. She was grateful that Cameron had taken a moment to move her train out of the way.

"I'm next level happy," Calvin responded to everyone's tell-tale glass clinking with a kiss that almost made her forget she was in a room full of people.

The entire night was amazing. Calvin stepped away to have a conversation and accepted the personal commendations of his brother Kings and Knights. Avant, wearing a tailored black suit, approached Mia.

"Congratulations." Avant gave her a hug. "I hope that I'll be lucky enough to find a love like yours."

"How's Toya and Leticia?" Mia didn't miss how Calvin's eyes locked onto hers. He made his way across the ballroom.

Avant's smile faltered. "They're currently staying with me until Leticia finds a job."

That explained a lot. Leticia's need for money made her a perfect mark. Mia had heard that Leticia's boyfriend had been arrested in connection with Gabriel's illegal activities. "Toya probably loves being in the house with you."

"Sorry." Calvin slid his arm around Mia's waist and smiled at Avant. "I have to steal *my wife* away." Without even allowing Avant time to protest, he guided Mia outside.

"You don't trust me," she teased.

"I trust *you* all day long," he answered. "Him? Not one damn bit."

Mia leaned on the banister, looking across the lake as she laughed.

He wrapped his arms around her. "Was it everything you hoped."

"More. Even more." Mia turned and faced him.

He reached into his inner pocket, retrieving what appeared to be a handkerchief. "I have a gift for you." Calvin placed the material in her hands.

"What's this?" Mia looked down. "A protection pod."

"All proceeds from the sale of this device go to building wealth for our children and their children."

"So the profit is not being re-invested into new inventions?" Mia smiled, shocked. He always put ninety percent of what he earned back into his next creations. This move right here said so much.

"No." Calvin slid his hand over her stomach. "We're laying the foundation for the Atwood family to make an impact on people's lives for years to come."

The day was more amazing than she could have ever dreamed. Mia was excited for the future. Life with Calvin and his inventions was sure to be a wild adventure. She prayed that their family would always be blessed by grace, grounded in divine wisdom, and rooted in eternal love

About the Author

National bestselling author, Karen D. Bradley, has penned several contemporary fiction, suspense, psychological thrillers, and romantic suspense. She has also contributed short stories to the Sugar anthology and the *Just One Kiss* anthology. Venturing into film making, she wrote and produced a short film based on one of her novels. Visit Karen on the web at www.karendbradley.com

About the *Knights of the Castle* Series

Don't miss the hot new standalone series. The Kings of the Castle made them family, but the Knights will transform the world.

Book 1 - King of Durabia – Naleighna Kai

No good deed goes unpunished, or that's how Ellena Kiley feels after she rescues a child and the former Crown Prince of Durabia offers to marry her.

Kamran learns of a nefarious plot to undermine his position with the Sheikh and jeopardize his ascent to the throne. He's unsure how Ellena, the fiery American seductress, fits into the plan but she's a secret weapon he's unwilling to relinquish.

Ellena is considered a sister by the Kings of the Castle and her connection to Kamran challenges her ideals, her freedoms, and her heart. Plus, loving him makes her a potential target for his enemies. When Ellena is kidnapped, Kamran is forced to bring in the Kings.

In the race against time to rescue his woman and defeat his enemies, the kingdom of Durabia will never be the same.

Book 2 - Knight of Bronzeville – Naleighna Kai and Stephanie M. Freeman

Chaz Maharaj thought he could maintain the lie of a perfect marriage for his adoring fans … until he met Amanda.

The connection between them should have ended with that unconditional "hall pass" which led to one night of unbridled passion. But once would never satisfy his hunger for a woman who could never be his. When Amanda walked out of his life, it was supposed to be forever. Neither of them could have anticipated fate's plan.

Chaz wants to explore his feelings for Amanda, but Susan has other ideas. Prepared to fight for his budding romance and navigate a plot that's been laid to crush them, an unexpected twist threatens his love and her life.

When Amanda's past comes back to haunt them, Chaz enlists the Kings of the Castle to save his newfound love in a daring escape.

Book 3 - Knight of South Holland – Karen D. Bradley

He's a brilliant inventor, but he'll decimate anyone who threatens his woman.

When the Kings of the Castle recommend Calvin Atwood, strategic defense inventor, to create a security shield for the kingdom of Durabia, it's the opportunity of a lifetime. The only problem—it's a two-year assignment and he promised his fiancée they would step away from their dangerous lifestyle and start a family.

Security specialist, Mia Jakob, adores Calvin with all her heart, but his last assignment put both of their lives at risk. She understands how important this new role is to the man she loves, but the thought that he may be avoiding commitment does cross her mind.

Calvin was sure he'd made the best decision for his and Mia's future, until enemies of the state target his invention and his woman. Set on a collision course with hidden foes, this Knight will need the help of the Kings to save both his Queen and the Kingdom of Durabia.

Book 4 - Lady of Jeffrey Manor – J. S. Cole and Naleighna Kai

He's the kingdom's most eligible bachelor. She's a practical woman on temporary assignment.

When surgical nurse, Blair Swanson, departed the American Midwest for an assignment in the Kingdom of Durabia she had no intention of finding love.

As a member of the royal family, Crown Prince Hassan has a responsibility to the throne. A loveless, arranged marriage is his duty, but the courageous American nurse is his desire.

When a dark secret threatens everything Hassan holds dear, how will he fulfill his royal duty and save the lady who holds his heart?

Book 5 - Knight of Grand Crossing – Hiram Shogun Harris, Naleighna Kai, and Anita L. Roseboro

Rahm did time for a crime he didn't commit. Now that he's free, taking care of the three women who supported him on a hellish journey is his priority, but old enemies are waiting in the shadows.

Rahm Fosten's dream life as a Knight of the Castle includes Marilyn Spears, who quiets the injustice of his rough past, but in his absence a new foe has infiltrated his family.

Marilyn Spears waited for many years to have someone like Rahm in her life. Now that he's home, an unexpected twist threatens to rip him away again. As much as she loves him, she's not willing to go where this new drama may lead.

Meanwhile, Rahm's gift to his Aunt Alyssa brings her to Durabia, where she catches the attention of wealthy surgeon, Ahmad Maharaj. Her attendance at a private Bliss event puts her under his watchful eye, but also in the crosshairs of the worst kind of enemy. Definitely the wrong timing for the rest of the challenges Rahm is facing.

While Rahm and Marilyn navigate their romance, a deadly threat has him and the Kings of the Castle primed to keep Marilyn, Alyssa, and his family from falling prey to an adversary out for bloody revenge.

Book 6 - Knight of Paradise Island – J. L. Campbell

Someone is killing women and the villain's next target strikes too close to the Kingdom of Durabia.

Dorian "Ryan" Bostwick is a protector and he's one of the best in the business. When a King of the Castle assigns him to find his former lover, Aziza, he stumbles upon a deadly underworld operating close to the Durabian border.

Aziza Hampton had just rekindled her love affair with Ryan when a night out with friends ends in her kidnapping. Alone and scared, she must find a way to escape her captor and reunite with her lover.

In a race against time, Ryan and the Kings of the Castle follow ominous clues into the underbelly of a system designed to take advantage of the vulnerable. Failure isn't an option and Ryan will rain down hell on earth to save the woman of his heart.

Book 7 - Knight of Irondale – J. L Woodson, Naleighna Kai, and Martha Kennerson

Neesha Carpenter is on the run from a stalker ex-boyfriend, so why are the police hot on her trail?

Neesha escaped the madness of her previous relationship only to discover the Chicago Police have named her the prime suspect in her ex's shooting. With her life spinning out of control, she turns to the one man who's the biggest threat to her heart—Christian Vidal, her high school sweetheart.

Christian has always been smitten with Neesha's strength, intelligence and beauty. He offers her safe haven in the kingdom of Durabia and will do whatever it takes to keep her safe, even enlisting the help of the Kings of the Castle.

Neesha and Christian's rekindled flame burns hotter even as her stay in the country places the royal family at odds with the American government.

As mounting evidence points to Neesha's guilt, Christian must ask the hard question … is the woman he loves being framed or did she pull the trigger?

Book 8 - Knight of Birmingham – Lori Hays and MarZe Scott

Single mothers who are eligible for release, have totally disappeared from the Alabama justice system.

Women's advocate, Meghan Turner, has uncovered a disturbing pattern and she's desperate for help. Then her worse nightmare becomes a horrific reality when her friend goes missing under the same mysterious circumstances.

Rory Tannous has spent his life helping society's most vulnerable. When he learns of Meghan's dilemma, he takes it personal. Rory has his own tragic past and he'll utilize every connection, even the King of the Castle, to help this intriguing woman find her friend and the other women.

As Rory and Meghan work together, the attraction grows and so does the danger. The stakes are high and they will have to risk their love and lives to defeat a powerful adversary.

Book 9 - Knight of Penn Quarter – Terri Ann Johnson and Michele Sims

Following an undercover FBI sting operation that didn't go as planned, Agent Mateo Lopez is ready to put the government agency in his rearview mirror.

A confirmed workaholic, his career soared at the cost of his love life which had crashed and burned until mutual friends arranged a date with beautiful, sharp-witted, Rachel Jordan, a rising star at a children's social services agency.

Unlucky in love, Rachel has sworn off romantic relationships, but Mateo finds himself falling for her in more ways than one. When trouble brews in one of Rachel's cases, he does everything in his power to keep her safe—even if it means resorting to extreme measures.

Will the choices they make bring them closer together or cost them their lives?

About the Kings of the Castle Series

"Did you miss The Kings of the Castle? "They are so expertly crafted and flow so well between each of the books, it's hard to tell each is crafted by a different author. Very well done!" - Lori H..., Amazon and Goodreads

Each King book 2-9 is a standalone, NO cliffhangers

Book 1 – Kings of the Castle, the introduction to the series and story of King of Wilmette (Vikkas Germaine)

USA TODAY, New York Times, and National Bestselling Authors work together to provide you with a world you'll never want to leave. The Castle.

Fate made them brothers, but protecting the Castle, each other, and the women they love, will make them Kings. Their combined efforts to find the current Castle members responsible for the attempt on their mentor's life, is the beginning of dangerous challenges that will alter the path of their lives forever.

These powerful men, unexpectedly brought together by their pasts and current circumstances, will become a force to be reckoned with.

King of Chatham - Book 2 – London St. Charles

While Mariano "Reno" DeLuca uses his skills and resources to create safe havens for battered women, a surge in criminal activity within the Chatham area threatens the women's anonymity and security. When Zuri, an exotic Tanzanian Princess, arrives seeking refuge from an arranged marriage and its deadly consequences, Reno is now forced to relocate the women in the shelter, fend off unforeseen enemies of The Castle, and endeavor not to lose his heart to the mysterious woman.

King of Evanston - Book 3 - J. L. Campbell

Raised as an immigrant, he knows the heartache of family separation firsthand. His personal goals and business ethics collide when a vulnerable woman stands to lose her baby in an underhanded and profitable scheme crafted by powerful, ruthless businessmen and politicians who have nefarious ties to The Castle. Shaz and the Kings of the Castle collaborate to uproot the dark forces intent on changing the balance of power within The Castle and destroying their mentor. National Bestselling Author, J.L. Campbell presents book 3 in the Kings of the Castle Series, featuring Shaz Bostwick.

King of Devon - Book 4 - Naleighna Kai

When a coma patient becomes pregnant, Jaidev Maharaj's medical facility comes under a government microscope and media scrutiny. In the midst of the investigation, he receives a mysterious call from someone in his past that demands that more of him than he's ever been willing to give and is made aware of a dark family secret that will destroy the people he loves most.

King of Morgan Park - Book 5 - Karen D. Bradley

Two things threaten to destroy several areas of Daron Kincaid's life—the tracking device he developed to locate victims of sex trafficking and an inherited membership in a mysterious outfit called The Castle. The new developments set the stage to dismantle the relationship with a woman who's been trained to make men weak or put them on the other side of the grave. The secrets Daron keeps from Cameron and his inner circle only complicates an already tumultuous situation caused by an FBI sting that brought down his former enemies. Can Daron take on his enemies, manage his secrets and loyalty to the Castle without permanently losing the woman he loves?

King of South Shore - Book 6 - MarZe Scott

Award-winning real estate developer, Kaleb Valentine, is known for turning failing communities into thriving havens in the Metro Detroit area. His plans to rebuild his hometown neighborhood are dereailed with one phone call that puts Kaleb deep in the middle of an intense criminal investigation led by a detective who has a personal vendetta. Now he will have to deal with the ghosts of his past before they kill him.

King of Lincoln Park - Book 7 – Martha Kennerson

Grant Khambrel is a sexy, successful architect with big plans to expand his Texas Company. Unfortunately, a dark secret from his past could destroy it all unless he's willing to betray the man responsible for that success, and the woman who becomes the key to his salvation.

King of Hyde Park - Book 8 -Lisa Dodson

Alejandro "Dro" Reyes has been a "fixer" for as long as he could remember, which makes owning a crisis management company focused on repairing professional reputations the perfect fit. The same could be said of Lola Samuels, who is only vaguely aware of his "true" talents and seems to be oblivious to the growing attraction between them. His company, Vantage Point, is in high demand and business in the Windy City is booming. Until a mysterious call following an attempt on his mentor's life forces him to drop everything and accept a fated position with The Castle. But there's a hidden agenda and unexpected enemy that Alejandro doesn't see coming who threatens his life, his woman, and his throne.

King of Lawndale - Book 9 - Janice M. Allen

Dwayne Harper's passion is giving disadvantaged boys the tools to transform themselves into successful men. Unfortunately, the minute he steps up to take his place among the men he considers brothers, two things stand in his way: a political office that does not want the competition Dwayne's new education system will bring, and a well-connected former member of The Castle who will use everything in his power—even those who Dwayne mentors—to shut him down.

www.ingramcontent.com/pod-product-compliance
Lightning Source LLC
Chambersburg PA
CBHW010833250626
47157CB00010B/3274